MW00773279

MAGNETIC PULLS

MAGNETIC
PULLS

C. A. MICKELS

Magnetic Pulls

Book covers by Bobby Ivory, www.ivorycoastmedia.com

All rights reserved. Published by Primary Media Group

This is a work of fiction. Names, characters, places, and incidents either are the product of the author's imagination or are used fictitiously.

Library of Congress Control Number: 2023920168

ISBN: 979-8-9893421-1-2

Printed in the United States of America
Also available on digital platforms

www.magneticpulls.com

DEDICATION

To my nephews and nieces, we started with short stories. Now we have arrived with a journey through *Magnetic Pulls*. And the journey has just begun...

ACKNOWLEDGMENTS

A special thank you to Joyelle Johnson, Suzette Carter-Saulnier and Dorthy Huddleston for their literary support.

TABLE OF CONTENTS

CHAPTER 1

The Matthews

It was a normal school day at Crossings High School, with the exception that it was the last week and the last day of school before spring break. Throughout the first part of the day, students were somewhat restless, in fact, very restless . . . until they arrived in Mr. Matthews' science class.

Mr. Matthews was the best teacher in the whole school. His class was a very special place. A very special world. He motioned us to come into his world of science and solar systems. He motioned us to come into his world... that was far, far away.

Science came alive in Mr. Matthews' classroom. There was a seven-foot, colorful, larger-than-life, spectacular exhibit of Earth's entire solar system in front of the classroom. It featured all the planets of the universe with built-in 3-D details. The entire exhibit lit up and moved in full motion like a freight train. Every time I looked at that solar system exhibit in motion, I always wondered if I should be someplace else . . . like in another world.

One day while I was wondering and dreaming because his class made my mind move like that, a flaming, blue-fire teenage girl walked through the wall. Her body moved like a cloud. She just stood there observing our class. I didn't know what to think. Who was she? Where did she come from? How did she just walk through a wall and appear out of nowhere? Did anyone else see her? The last thing I needed was a visit from an unexpected being from another world. I was still trying to figure out my own world. Maybe she had some answers for my life; maybe she didn't.

Then she disappeared as quickly as she came. I was confused. I felt like my thoughts had gotten the best of me. What made matters worse was that I was the only one to see her that day. Suddenly I realized that it was just an illusion. Whew! That was good because I didn't need anything rocking my world, especially in my science class. Science was my refuge from the rest of the world.

During class, Mr. Matthews always found new ways to make science an adventure. We were told our science classroom setup, and projects could compete with the city's Natural Museum of Science, and we believed it.

One day two men dressed in the black National Science Foundation uniforms paid a visit to our science class. Something didn't seem quite right about their visit. Mr. Matthews appeared very nervous that day, too. He was never nervous when people popped in to observe his classes. In fact, he was always proud to show how great his classes and his students were. Supposedly, the two men came to see our class's science exhibits and to watch Mr. Matthews in action. But there was something very different about that day and that visit.

Mr. Matthews was twenty-five years old and fresh out of college. He looked younger than his age. We assumed he had graduated early. His complexion and short, dark brown hair made us think he was Italian. He also wore mountain climber boots a lot because he was a hiker. Kids liked being around Mr. Matthews. I thought he really liked being around us, too. Teaching didn't seem like a job to him. It was a sport, and we were his team. He was our coach, and he pushed us to give him our best. And we did. He believed in us, and that made us believe in ourselves.

Now, you might not believe what I'm about to tell you. I know that just about everyone has a brother or a sister. Well . . . I heard Mr. Matthews had a twin brother . . . an evil twin brother. You heard it right. The best teacher in the whole school had an evil twin brother. That's what they said. And they were identical twins.

Mr. Matthews' brother, Mervin, came to Crossings High School to teach first. Then, Mr. Matthews arrived a year later. Both twin brothers were hired as science teachers. Mervin Matthews was the physics teacher, and Mr. Matthews was the Earth science teacher. Mervin Matthews taught at Crossings for one whole year.

The talk is, Mervin was brilliant. He was a modern, young version of Albert Einstein. He had degrees in math, biology, and physical sciences. Everyone respected him; the principal, the teachers, the students, and especially the parents. They were proud to have a brainy teacher like him on staff. And he was obsessed with science.

Because Mervin Matthews was at the school first, the principal and the parents thought Mr. Matthews would follow in his brother's footsteps. But all the teachers, and especially the students, knew— Mr. Matthews and his twin brother were definitely different. However, when it came to science, there was no question about it. The Matthews twins had good science genes.

After his first year of teaching, Mervin Matthews was invited to NASA for a summer internship. Having a NASA internship in your portfolio was a high honor for any teacher, especially a twenty-five-year-old teacher. Rumor has it that Mr. Matthews' brother gained knowledge of some pretty high-level space research secrets at NASA that summer. When he came back to school at the end of the summer, he was acting really strange.

Rumor also has it . . . that while Mr. Matthews' brother was at NASA, he gained knowledge about an advanced species of teenagers. Another story has it…that after his return in the fall, he came back to school acting like there was a crisis in education and that students were falling short. Could it be that he was comparing us with teenagers from another world? Like maybe the advanced species he's supposed to have found out about? Was that too much information for a twenty-five-year-old? Was his mind able to handle all that research?

He seemed to have gone over the top. We all thought NASA went to his head, and he came back acting like he was in charge of the world. Just about everyone treated him like he was the chosen one. Chosen for what?

Mervin Matthews started conducting himself like he was a national science diplomat. If you didn't understand that, maybe you'll understand this. He was acting like a United States Navy Seal scientist, a special ops officer, or something. Overnight he thought he was a higher authority than our principal. The principal and the parents didn't recognize it at first, but the other teachers and we students did. Now . . . everything was about to unravel.

Mr. Matthews' brother thought he was above the other teachers, too. He picked up an "official look" of sorts. He no longer dressed like the other teachers. He started wearing all black: black designer turtle necks, black designer straight-leg pants, and black designer soft leather loafers. Every day was black attire for him. And he stood out even more when he changed his hairstyle. He went from dark brown, dry hair to jet black, gelled hair. The talk was he thought he was making a cool statement by setting himself apart from the other teachers, who dressed casually. But his attire looked like an Alaskan seal's outfit. What I mean is it clung to his body, and it looked like something you would wear to carry out a secret spy mission.

That wasn't even half of it. Mervin Matthews changed his teaching style, too. At first, it was so weird that it was funny, although no one had the nerve to laugh in his face. Then one day, he walked into his classroom and started strolling up and down the rows like a drill sergeant. In fact, if I'm not mistaken, he was sort of marching. And he was tapping his pencil on each student's desk as he walked up and down the rows.

He started hollering, "You students need to come up a few notches. You're not holding up your part of the bargain to learn science. You're going to put the entire country at risk."

And it got worse! He started giving kids class assignments that were impossible to finish in the time granted, and then he sped up the pace of the class. It got so bad that the class valedictorian had a meltdown!

The principal didn't mind him putting extra pressure on the students. He felt like Mervin Matthews was making up for the slack from summer, and so did the parents. Then all of a sudden, it all stopped . . . when three teenage boys went missing. The last place those boys were seen was in Mervin Matthews' class. After that, things became real quiet in our school. Kids became real scared, too. But instead of the craziness stopping, it continued.

One day some officers from the United States Air Force appeared at Crossings High and escorted Mr. Matthews' brother out of the school and off the school grounds. He was walking out like an honored government official. I didn't get it. Why was he being escorted out? And why by the United States Air Force? Who was in charge? Why weren't the school's security guards escorting him out? And why did our principal just stand in the hallway with his eyes bulging out like a turtle as Mervin was marching out like a head rooster? The principal looked scared to me, and he didn't wave good-bye to Mervin Matthews. Mr. Matthews' brother must have really received some real high-level government secrets at NASA for things to have changed overnight. Students weren't given an explanation for what happened or what didn't happen.

The rumors went wild! The first information source said that the school's principal was so afraid of him that when he finally got the nerve to fire Mervin Matthews, instead of having the school's security guards present, they called the Air Force to escort him out. It's just a rumor, and that's all we have to work with.

The second rumor has it that Mervin Matthews went to Washington, D.C., and talked with the president about some new teaching methods. It's highly unlikely that the president of the United States would meet with an over-the-top, young, frustrated science teacher... or would he?

One student was heard confidently proclaiming, "He's still on NASA's payroll."

The student was probably paid to say that. That *couldn't* be true!!

Our science teacher, Mr. Matthews, *never* talks about his brother or his incidents. He keeps a real low profile. I don't blame him. People just assume things when you are closely related. They assume you

7

are the same. You experience that a lot when you have brothers and sisters.

In-person, Mr. Matthews' brother, Mervin, appeared real presentable and professional. The students knew that he was extreme, but they were unable to prove it and get away with it. When students tried to complain about his teaching style, they always ended up looking crazy. It didn't matter how smart they were.

Once, Mr. Matthews' brother overheard a student comment that he hadn't taken time to study for a test, so Mervin Mathews took matters into his own hands. The next day he gave the student an experiment that turned his face, arms, and hands blue for three days. The student walked around looking like a bluebird. When he finally went to the hospital, the doctors couldn't figure out whether he was sick or crazy. One thing, though, they never discovered what caused the student to turn blue.

In another episode, he underhandedly set up a special electricity assignment where a student got slightly shocked. It was no coincidence that the same student had complained about his teaching methods earlier. Why couldn't he just be like his brother, Mr. Matthews, and make science and learning fun?

Unlike Mervin Matthews, Mr. Matthews' life was teaching. He was a good teacher, the best, to be exact. When people do what they love and they are good at it, my mother always says that they're in their "calling." I wondered why she didn't just say they were gifted or talented like a baseball player, an artist, or a doctor. Everyone is good at something, I guess.

Anyway, Mr. Matthews' science class was the best part of my school day, and science had become a major part of my life. It helped me to understand the world, although I still hadn't figured out where I fit in. I am getting close, though. But remember, I am just a teen-ager, so I still have a lot of time to put my life together.

CHAPTER 2

Spring Break

My parents think I'm just a kid transitioning to an adult. Sometimes they say I move back and forth between being a kid and an adult. Both positions have their advantages and disadvantages. Right now, I am right in the middle . . . just analyzing life and trying to figure things out. My life is composed of my teachers, my family, my three friends, my phone, and, of course, my video games. Our school is so large that everyone and everything else is just a spectacle.

Every day I sit next to the same students in science class, Madison and Austin. They are my best friends. What makes us friends is that we have a lot in common. For one, we're from the same small, out-of-the-way neighborhood and the same small school. So, we've all known each other for a long time. Most of the other kids come from large schools and lots of different neighborhoods. Now that we're all teenagers, they say it doesn't matter what neighborhood or school you're from anymore. But we still feel that it does matter, and it makes a difference. And that's why the three of us stick together.

Ever since Austin had a dream about those three missing boys from Mervin Matthews' class, he has been sticking even closer to

Madison and me. Austin has this false impression that he might be next on Mr. Matthews' brother's list. He didn't do anything wrong, and I told him over and over again not to worry. It was just a dream. He finally took my advice and stopped worrying, but he still reports his whereabouts to us all the time.

Austin, like most people, dreams at night. I, on the other hand, have daydreams; some call it imagination. Last Tuesday, right in the middle of class, my imagination started to run wild. It was kind of like Austin's dream but in a different way. I began to wonder what had really happened to the three boys that disappeared from our school. It was hard to try to blame Mr. Matthews' twin brother for their disappearance.

Everybody knew they had some issues, like skipping class. Plus, one or two of them were known to stay in trouble. They were always in the principal's office. But that's still no reason to stop being concerned about them. It was hard to believe that something really bad had happened to them, especially since their so-called disappearance never showed up on the local news.

The missing boys were a threesome, always together, kind of like Madison, Austin, and me. By the way, has anyone seen them in their neighborhood lately? There was one suspicious thing, though. Since their disappearance, American flags have been flying high outside the boys' homes . . . and the flags weren't there before. We all know they couldn't have joined the military. They were too young.

Maybe the three boys received permission to leave early for spring break. *Maybe* their disappearance had something to do with Mervin Matthews' "government top secret." Or it could be they joined that new, advanced species of teenagers that he supposedly got some inside info about on his trip to NASA. Here's another strange thing: Mervin Matthews hasn't surfaced yet, either. Maybe he found a job teaching science in South America or Alaska.

I wonder if that new species of teenagers' bodies have bones.

Anyway, getting back to my friends and continuing on . . . Madison, Austin, and I are gamers. We are not obsessed with video games, but we are good at them. For the record, we are some of the best gamers in school. Without question, we are the best in our grade. Gaming isn't just fun. It's a way to get respect. Madison is a gamer . . . and a good one. That's a rare quality for a girl. She also likes to sing, and she's good at that, too. She's the kind of girl that might show up on a TV talent show one day. She is just working up her nerve and perfecting her talent. The three of us manage to stay out of trouble in school and at home. In fact, all three of us get good grades.

Not everyone likes gaming. A lot of parents think video games are the enemy. Some adults have even gone so far as to produce research studies against video game usage. The research studies say that excessive video game usage damages kids' brain cells. Well, whatever happened to the research studies about excessive television viewing?

TV is passive. Games are active and action-packed. Hmmmm. I smell game haters.

Overall, most teachers aren't game haters. They just want to make sure there's more time for learning. Because the law is on their side, and school learning time is guaranteed, they *are* willing to bargain with students. Besides, teachers know students need mental breaks. They're looking for mental breaks themselves. Lucky for *all* of us, spring break was just around the corner.

We're one day away from spring break. I'm excited because my pal and friend, Gabe, who lives in South America, is coming to visit me tomorrow. To be exact, he's coming from a rural town in Brazil. I can hardly wait. I'm going to put my best foot forward for America and show him the best time of his life.

Gabe has always dreamed of coming to America. He loves fast things. And he heard that things move fast, like lightning in America, and we have train rides in the skies. He carries around one small, pre-owned video game in his pocket. To most Americans, his game is outdated, but for him, it's the latest. That's why he can't wait to get to America. He dreams about playing the latest American video games.

Now, don't think for one moment that Gabe's life in Brazil is bad. When he's not in school, he's surfing the ocean every day or exploring the best forests and jungles in Brazil.

13

I couldn't wait for Gabe to meet my friends. Thinking about it was exciting. I felt like this would be our best spring break ever. My father gave me some extra cash to entertain my house guest. As soon as I get out of school, I'm heading straight to a game store to get the latest and the best games for us to play. Class isn't out yet, and spring break hasn't begun, so in the meantime, I better pay attention in class because Mr. Matthews doesn't tolerate slacking off.

The classroom lights are dim. Mr. Matthews is about to do a live science illustration - again. There are two displays in the front of the class. The second display is a large magnet with two poles. The poles are generating magnetic fields. The magnetic fields are pulling objects before our eyes.

"Today we're going to talk about magnets," Mr. Matthews announced.

Then he walked over to the massive solar system exhibit and pointed to the Sun. One part of our class's solar system display showed the Sun functioning as a magnet with all the planets circulating around it.

"The Sun acts like a giant magnet," he said. "Magnetism is one of the basic forces of nature."

Then he rushed over to the magnetic display.

"Magnetic fields can pull objects toward one pole or another pole," he continued. "There are two kinds of magnets: permanent magnets and electromagnets. Can someone give me an example of a permanent magnet?"

Madison shouted, "Mars is a permanent magnet."

"Someone else, give me an example of where an electromagnet is used. Anton."

"Electromagnets are used in electronics, like video games and computers."

"Right," Mr. Matthews said. "Remember the magnetic pulls,"

Spring break starts tomorrow. In Mr. Matthews' mind, learning never stops. That's why he took the liberty of giving us a class project over the break. He always says that science never stops. It's part of life. Look at it that way, and it won't seem like work.

The dismissal bell rings. Most of the kids rush out of the room and out of the building like it's a fire drill. I walk out like it's my birthday. . . I'm heading straight to a game store.

In the commotion, Mr. Matthews hollers, "Remember your science projects over the break. Austin is running toward me. I really didn't know why.

"Anton, hold up. Mr. Matthews' twin brother has surfaced!"

"What!" I shouted.

"Yeah, and I just heard he opened a new video store with the latest games from all around the world."

I was in shock as I questioned Austin.

"He owns a new video store!?! Are you kidding me!?"

"Nope!" Austin replied. "Mr. Matthews' brother must have some pull with *some*body."

"He must," I said, not really knowing whether or not I believed it.

Austin was really on a roll now. He could hardly control his excitement.

"He's supposed to have created his own video games, too. Get this. They say there's a special section of his video game store called the 'The Back Room'. Inside 'The Back Room' is an enormous, bright green, fluorescent sign that reads '*Video Games of the Future*'. It's supposed to be the best video game store in town."

"Really?" I said. "Wow! Then, who cares if he's a little crazy? I'm going to check it out. My friend, Gabe, from South America, will be here tomorrow . . . and I need some new games."

In amazement, Austin replied, "Sooo . . . Mervin Matthews' next move was a game store for youth. Can you believe that? That must have been in the works for a long time. How do you go from teaching science to owning a large game store?"

"Consider the source," I said. "This guy has secrets. Let a twenty-five-year-old hotshot into NASA, and he comes back with games."

As Austin and I approached the new game store, we saw kids standing everywhere.

In unbelief, Austin said, "There is actually a line to get into this place? This is unheard of. It's not even Christmas. It's not even a new game day."

The inside and outside of the game store looked like a school field trip outing without parents or teachers. There were kids everywhere.

Looking around, I told Austin, "Well . . . I guess he got his class back."

Once we were inside, we understood what all the excitement was about.

Austin commented, "This is a high-tech, international game store, something right out of a sci-fi movie!"

He was right. There were video games from just about every country in the world. You name it. China, Japan, South Korea, Brazil, and, of course, America.

With a sense of certainty in his voice, Austin said, "This place has got to be one of a kind. It looks like a trial station for new games."

I continued to wonder. *What did Mervin Matthews have to do with this store?* We hadn't seen him yet, as we walked around. But what we *did* see were three men who were dressed in the same black, seal-looking outfits that Mr. Matthews' brother wore. Their outfits were kind of retro and really cool.

All three of the men looked like they were old enough to go to college but not young enough to be in high school. One looked

Asian. Another looked African American, and the other one sounded like he might have been European. Two of them had a noticeable accent. They didn't look like your regular, minimum-wage, retail help, either. Instead, they looked like research scientists. Go figure.

Word was going around that these three men were actually former science teachers, but what business were they doing with Mr. Matthews' brother? Anyway, what's up with these serious-looking dudes in high-tech, black outfits? This is a video game store. At least, we thought it was a game store—until we entered into the innermost back room. That's the second room where you find all the games of the future. Once we had gotten over the thrill of being there, I began to understand the seriousness of it all. Video games had become big business.

Suddenly, Mervin Matthews walked through the door before we could get another word out of our mouths. I'm not psychic, but I knew it was him because he looked just like Mr. Matthews, with the exception of a few things. He had a crazy look in his eyes . . . on edge . . . like something was bothering him.

To our surprise, he approached us and said, "What are you looking for?"

"Fighting games," I answered.

After looking us up and down, he replied, "Same games . . . companies . . . games. That's all you kids ever want. Are you up for trying something new? Real new?"

He took a step forward and moved closer to us as if he was about to whisper something. Austin was comfortable with his advance toward us. I wasn't, and you know why! So I took a step backward from him.

"Someone just shipped me some new games. Follow me," he said.

We followed him to the other side of the room. Austin was looking around like he was watching his back because he *still* didn't want to be the fourth missing kid. Mervin Matthews removed a game off the shelf. It was called "Aquatic Warlords." He was about to hand it over to us . . . he hesitated, stopped, and asked us a few questions.

"What kind of students are you? Do you know anything about aquatic life, the ocean, or the seas? How much do you know about science?"

A few thoughts went through my head, but I didn't say them out loud. *What kind of teacher were you? A game is a game. Where's this guy coming from?*

I answered, "It's still a fighting game."

He replied, "*This* game might be a little bit more aggressive than what you are accustomed to. You are going to have to use your instincts and scientific knowledge to survive."

He was speaking calmly. He was trying to come across like a nice guy. I can take a challenge. So I took his game. After he recommended the first game I asked him if he would recommend a second one. He smiled at us as if he was glad to have another chance to help us. His smile didn't move me.

"I have just the game for you," he said. "It's in the fourth dimension."

"What's that?" I asked.

"It's like playing outside the known universe," he responded.

After he said that, he just kind of grinned to himself. The game looked interesting and fun. "OK. I'll try it," I said.

The second game was called "Solar System Stretch". A space galaxy was on the cover of the package. The back cover had a few directions. I didn't think that much about it . . . although I should have.

Before I could walk away, he said, "There's one important thing I need to explain to you about these games. They don't operate with the normal hand-held controllers. These controllers are strapped to your wrists and hands."

My thoughts started running wild. *Strapped? That sounds crazy. What's going on?*

Then he continued.

"They need to be attached to your body at all times. The controllers are activated by your hands, words, and thoughts."

"How many controllers are included in our game?" I asked.

"Five hand-wrist controllers are included in the game. Make certain you read the directions carefully."

Then he said it a second time.

But this time, he fixed his eyes directly on us and pronounced every word with authority.

"Read c-a-r-e-f-u-l-l-y and f-o-l-l-o-w the directions."

There appeared to be a second message behind his eyes and words that he wasn't communicating. I guess it was for him to know and for us to find out. I thanked Mervin Matthews for his help.

Then he shook my hand and said, "Welcome to the games of the future. I'll see you when you return."

We walked over to the cash register, and I purchased the games.

As the cashier was bagging our purchases, he looked up at me and said, "There's a bonus game for every game of the future purchased this week."

The cashier slipped the bonus game into our bag real quick. Something about it appeared suspicious to me. Consider the landscape: four former science teachers . . . all dressed in the same black outfits . . . from four seemingly different countries . . . selling video games to kids. Question. Why did they leave teaching? Why were they selling video games to kids? What's the connection? I hope that friendly-looking cashier didn't put a secret tracking monitor in my bag.

CHAPTER 3

Spyglass to the Skies

Spring break had started, and as soon as Gabe arrived in America, things began to move real fast.

For six months, I had known that my long-distance friend was coming to America for spring break. I could imagine he was counting down the days, just like me. I guess he felt like I felt when I was five years old and my parents told me I was going to Disney World for the first time. In my mind, it was like going to a castle in the sky, a place of fantasy and great expectations. Well, today, Gabe was coming to America, a place of fantasy and expectations for him!

Gabe loved fast things, and he was about to experience the fastest ride of his life and his very first airplane ride. This was it; the trip of a lifetime. It wasn't just the trip. It was the thrill of the ride in the plane . . . on its way to America!

After the plane landed, the captain did something special. He handed Gabe his very own pilot's hat as a souvenir. That one act of kindness and his overall flight to America changed the course of Gabe's life forever.

My father picked me up from school, and we headed to the airport to pick Gabe up. We were at the arrival gate. Although I wasn't sure I would recognize him, I did have an old picture he had emailed me some time ago. As soon as he walked through the security gate and we made eye contact with each other, we kind of immediately knew who we were. Gabe walked over to my dad and me. We greeted each other with two shoulder brushes like old friends do.

Before I could speak, Gabe announced, "I am here!"

My dad just grinned and asked, "How was your flight?"

Gabe skipped his flight question and belted out, "USA! USA!" in his Portuguese accent.

"Oh! I almost forgot something," he added.

He went into his backpack and proudly pulled out a small Brazilian flag, and handed it to my father. Right away, I could tell my father liked him.

Gabe and I have a lot in common. For one, we both speak English and Spanish, although his native language is Portuguese. Language isn't the only thing we have in common. We both like games and astronomy. We've learned that there is no distance when it comes to friendship. We've managed to share our interests over the years, either through emails or text messages, or social media.

Our friendship started in an international exchange program two years ago. American students were paired with students from other countries. They exchanged living situations with each other. The program allowed the students to learn about and experience each other's cultures and learn to communicate outside their own world. For what we were about to experience, these skills would prove to be quite valuable.

We arrived at my house, and as soon as Gabe put his suitcase down in my bedroom, the doorbell rang. I looked out the bedroom window to see who it was. To my surprise, I saw that a delivery man in a large, white, unmarked commercial truck was sitting a huge package down at the front door. The huge package had one name on it... mine. I wasn't expecting any packages, and definitely not any big ones. So you can imagine my surprise.

The delivery man had on an outfit that I recognized right away, even though I didn't see his face. It was a black, seal-looking outfit. To be exact, he was wearing a clinging, black turtleneck with black, straight-legged pants. And . . . he had black gelled hair. As soon as my mother opened the door, the delivery man dashed back into the truck and drove off.

After we dragged the package into the house, my family watched in anticipation as I cut open the "mystery" package. Once I got it open and saw the contents, I found the surprise of a lifetime, a powerful space telescope! Some mysterious person had sent me my very own telescope. Now, this wasn't a telescope for beginners or even for somebody at an intermediate level, and it wasn't a toy. It was the real thing! It was a *professional* astronomer's telescope.

It was computerized with a GPS. It was able to look at deep-space objects that were otherwise completely hidden. It even had software that allowed you to automatically find celestial bodies. There were over one hundred definable objects already programmed for us to see. With a push of a button, my eyes were on the red, rocky surface of Mars.

I decided to name my telescope "Spyglass to the Skies." My parents didn't know quite how to interpret this big-ticket item from a mysterious sender. Who would send a pricey telescope to a teenager? I knew it was valuable. There was no receipt attached, and there wasn't a bill, so everything was fine with me. We didn't even get a notification that a package was coming.

I didn't have a problem receiving a gift. Christmas was over, and my family was on a tight budget. My father had made an exception for my new video game purchases. He thought it was real important to show our houseguest a good time while he was in America. My father didn't object to me keeping the gift. He was just curious about the sender. I didn't have a second thought about it. I was too excited about the telescope.

The weather station had forecast clear skies for tonight. That meant we would have a front-row seat to the skies. This professional telescope was about to work for us tonight.

Up to now, I had only had small telescopes, but *this* telescope put me in another league, on another level, out of the box, and over the top!! Gabe was about to experience it with me.

"Do you know what this is?" I asked him.

"Yes, it's a professional telescope. I've worked with them before," he said.

I was surprised at his response. His knowledge of telescopes, the universe, the galaxies, and the sky was a lot more than I had anticipated. You can never rule out a person's knowledge based upon where they are from. Knowledge, learning, and experience are free . . . and available to everyone.

In my limited thinking, I assumed that he had never visited any observatories or large city museums, but I was seriously mistaken. How could I come up with a misguided thought like that? I have never been to Brazil. Had I paid closer attention in geography class, I would have remembered that Brazil was the largest country in South America. Besides, Gabe and I have always shared our love for science and astronomy through our emails over the years.

Gabe once told me about an experience he had one night while at home. He had looked up into the midnight sky and saw what appeared to be shooting stars from every direction. In reality, it turned out to be a meteor shower. When he first saw it, he didn't know what to think.

He explained that he had never seen anything like that before. At first, he thought about running but then decided to just keep watching the sky. He said that the meteors looked like white, shiny swords flashing through space into Earth's midnight sky. The long, electric-looking swords were coming from everywhere. The dashing streaks of light appeared to be the size of a human body, and their appearance changed as they moved closer to Earth.

Shortly after the meteor experience, Gabe explained that he made it his business to find out all he could about what was going on in space. So he found his way to an observatory that had a professional telescope.

Once in our emails, Gabe wrote that he thought there might be other planets like Earth somewhere in space. I thought so, too. If there were other planets, there might be other people *on* those planets.

As Gabe and I were observing the planets with my new telescope, something totally unexpected happened. We thought we saw a human figure on Mars. At least it had the *outline* of a human figure. I saw it first; then Gabe saw it. Our imaginations started racing. It was hard to tell if it was just our hopes or reality. When we tried to concentrate on the person, the image, or whatever the figure was, it moved outside of our vision field and hid like it knew it was being watched.

Mars is rocky, with reddish-orange canyons and mountains. The figure kept moving in and out of our sight by running behind the mountains and into the canyons. It was easy to spot because it was a shimmering, bluish-white color, almost like blue mouthwash. It stood out against the backdrop of Mars' dark mountains. It appeared as if it was playing hide-and-seek with us. We waited for the slim, shimmering human figure to return, but it disappeared.

The human figure was not a shadow. It was something that was definitely alive. It was light and airy, and it moved with ease in somewhat of a delightful way. It was the height of a human being, with a small, shimmering shape like a girl, and it dashed about with human-like movements. Maybe it was a living thing that was alien to our world. I doubt it. We witnessed it with our own eyes.

This human figure wasn't part of the telescope. Gabe and I went to work to prove it. We examined the telescope's lens; it was clear. We checked the brand name and the construction of the telescope on the internet. It *was* the real thing.

The mystifying, shimmering figure did not return, at least not at that moment. So we went on to explore the other one hundred celestial images. Venus, Mercury, the stars, the Milky Way, the moon, Neptune, and Saturn were all exciting and breathtaking. As our eyes moved through each celestial body, we felt like we were daydreaming at night. But it was nothing compared to the light and airy, shimmering human figure our eyes had just seen.

I couldn't wait to tell Austin and Madison about the new telescope I had received and the dashing, blue human figure that Gabe and I had spotted on Mars. This was hot news. I also couldn't wait for them to meet Gabe. They were on their way over to start the science project that Mr. Matthews had given to us to work on during spring break. But that was just a small indication of what their visit would prove to be.

Maybe the sketchy figure on Mars just showed up for us. Maybe it wanted to send a message back to Earth. Who's to say if we were the first human beings to see him, her, or whatever it was?

Good things usually happen whenever Austin, Madison, and I are together. This time the team was juggling two balls up in the air: our science project and new video games. We were about to figure out that the new telescope had created a shortcut for us to finish our science project in less than half the time. Before we got down to business, I introduced Gabe to my team. Gabe fit right in. He liked them, and they liked him.

Then I showed them the telescope. They were fascinated and couldn't stop talking about it. Like me, Gabe was waiting patiently for Madison and Austin to get past the excitement of the telescope so we could move on with the games. They were amazed with the telescope's ability to zero in on over one hundred defined objects in the night sky. They were so excited that they forgot to ask where it came from. Something else happened, too. It didn't take long for us to figure out that this new telescope was our ticket to victory in our science project.

Madison took the lead and put the project together. She decided we could use the photographic software to take pictures of the telescope's top twenty most spectacular celestial sites in the sky. It was a no-brainer. Each celestial body had been programmed and had a two-paragraph write-up in the telescope's introduction book, so much for research. The write-ups would be our written presentation.

I didn't forget to tell Madison and Austin about the mysterious figure, but instead of telling them directly, Gabe and I decided to take another course of action. We wanted them to discover the phenomenon on their own, just like we did. We wanted to see their initial reaction to the figure, even though we weren't even sure that it would appear. So, we had Madison position herself behind the eyepiece. Boy, was it worth the wait!

As Madison was looking through the telescope, Gabe whispered to me, "We're dealing with an unpredictable space creature. There is a possibility Austin and Madison might see a different figure than what we saw. The creature might even respond in another way."

"Well," I whispered back. "One thing I know for certain about Madison. She has a way with people. People really open up and relax around her. Let's just watch to see what happens when she looks through the telescope."

Madison was on a roll with the telescope. She was trying to view every major celestial object. She had just started on the letter "M" when she reached Mars. Like us, she journeyed through the volcanoes and mountains and was astonished at the red appearance of the planet.

Then she screamed and yelled, "Is there a volume button on this telescope?"

"For what?" I asked.

"I didn't know there was life on Mars! I see what looks like a girl! And she's dancing and singing! Someone's dancing and singing on Mars! Hmmm. Now . . . I *really* want to know what she's singing."

While the "mystery girl" held Madison's complete attention, we found the volume button. We turned it up loud and heard her singing joyfully with her whole heart.

"Do you wanna dance? Now watch me dance. Do you wanna sing? Now watch me sing. Do you wanna move? Now watch me move."

"This is *crazy*!" I said. "A girl dancing on Mars?!? Why did she decide to dance and sing to Madison?"

Gabe responded, "Well, you said people open up to Madison. I guess you were right."

The sound of the mysterious girl's voice expressed pure joy. Her joy was contagious. Madison was always quick on her feet. She did the right thing. She snapped a picture of the girl from Mars dancing and singing with joy.

Austin was determined to see the dancing mystery girl, so he took his next-in-line rights from Madison for the telescope. He caught the last move of her dancing. Then she stopped. We are not certain whether the camera flash caused her to stop dancing or whether it was the appearance of Austin. In any case, she immediately stopped and vanished behind the red caves, and that was the last we saw of her for a while.

For a moment, we just looked at each other in unbelief. Gabe and I didn't see her dancing, but we didn't have to. We heard her singing . . . and it was for real! Gabe was right. The mystery creature was unpredictable, and she did react in a different way with Madison and Austin. It wasn't enough that we had a picture of the "mystery girl from Mars". I had to ask Madison some questions.

"What did you see? What did she look like to you?"

"She was a teenage girl who seemed to be real happy and full of life. She was dancing with rhythm and ease. She was a pretty good dancer, too. She kept moving her body from side to side and back and forth."

"Was it like American dancing?"

"Kind of. Her body appeared almost transparent, but it wasn't. It was a shimmering, bluish-white color.

"How could you tell she was a girl?"

"Her body structure and her hair, even though her hair looked like blue fire. Do you know what was really strange? Although she was different from us, she seemed like a typical teenage girl."

It was time to work on our science project. But it *was* hard. The dancing girl from Mars had made us lose our Earthly focus. Although Madison was listening to Austin and Gabe talk, she had a faraway look. I think she was really thinking about the girl on Mars. I wondered if it dawned on her that the girl seemed to instinctively pick up that Madison liked to sing, dance, and perform.

I wondered if she had extra-terrestrial mental powers. She seemed to have read Madison's thoughts. Maybe she read her mind because she liked Madison and wanted to be friends with her. *But how can you pick a new friend millions of miles away?* Austin and Gabe had a theory about the mystery girl that sounded interesting. Their theory was connected to magnetic pulls.

Gabe said, "I believe the mysterious girl from Mars received a magnetic pull from Madison. The magnetic pull triggered an inward response that prompted her to sing and dance."

My only comment about Gabe and Austin's theory was, "If it's a real magnetic pull, who is pulling who? And what's next?"

The night was late. In the midst of our excitement about outer space, it was time for Madison and Austin to go home. So they departed, and Gabe and I spent the rest of the night dreaming and wondering if we would ever see the "mystery girl" again. I'm sure Madison and Austin were dreaming and wondering, too.

CHAPTER 4

Aquatic Warlords

The second day of spring break began. Madison and Austin were home, and Gabe and I were about to play our first video game from the game store. We couldn't wait to get started. What delights and adventures lay ahead of us? We couldn't begin to imagine.

Besides being smart, Gabe was used to staying busy. He was eager and excited about playing. So it was time to start playing video games. I started him off at the beginner's level. He went from a beginner to an intermediate level real fast. His concentration was unbelievable. I think it's because teenagers in other countries have better concentration. Maybe it's because they don't have as many distractions as American teens. Whatever the reason, Gabe caught on fast with his computer-like mind. He was very, very smart.

The second day, we played video games non-stop for five straight hours. It was a marathon. Gabe mastered the controllers and the games easily. By the end of the afternoon, I knew he would be a pro. We hadn't gotten around to Mervin Matthews' games yet, but now we were ready to play them. We needed two minds to figure out one game. Mervin Matthews' games required a different mindset, a paradigm shift, and a totally different way of thinking and playing at the same time.

When we started, we thought it was a game. We had no idea it would be another world, too. Maybe this game was part of Mervin Matthews' high-level, government secret mission. I started to remember some of the things that he had said about the games and his directions for them.

Interestingly, he had kept muttering, over and over, "Your words have power. You create life by your words. Words have energy."

It was obvious that the words that he had spoken had more meaning than we cared to understand. We only wanted to play a game, not start a new world order. However, for some reason, we did decide to watch our words. What he said did have an effect on us. After all, he knew the games a lot better than we did. And, obviously, he knew something *about* the games that we didn't know, either.

I remember hearing someone once say, "Life and death are in the power of your words."

Even though I didn't understand what it meant, it always stayed with me. But for what we were about to experience, Mervin Matthews could have at least given us a few more clues.

Gabe was fascinated by American video games and how easy it was to find them and buy them in America.

"Where did you get these games, Anton?"

"I purchased them from a science teacher who turned into a video gamer."

"Really?!? That doesn't ever happen in Brazil."

"It usually doesn't happen in America, either. I think he just slipped through the cracks during his background check for teaching. Just joking."

With a puzzled look on his face, Gabe said slowly, "Ok, so teachers are opening up game stores here? That's really different."

I wasn't about to try and explain our school system. And even though I knew nothing about how teachers got hired, I think the school might have overlooked some things in Mervin Matthews' case. Now, that's just my opinion.

We started the game, "Aquatic Warlords." We strapped the controllers onto our wrists and pushed the start button. In seconds we found ourselves tumbling through a glowing, white portal into another world. Once we passed through the portal, we found ourselves in the flow of a swift ocean current. Struggling not to drown and swimming as best we could, we focused on keeping our heads above the water. We kicked and stroked as we gulped for air. The rushing ocean current carried us a ways and then finally propelled us upward toward the Sunlight Zone, the top layer of the ocean. At that point, we gave up struggling and just rode the current.

We were about a football field's length from the surface of the chilling, blue ocean, and we could see the sun's rays beaming down and going through the water. We were close to the sun and close to the surface of the ocean at the same time, but the football field's length was very deep. It's even deep for a boat, although we weren't in one. We still had a ways to go, so we just let the current carry us.

Before we knew it, an ocean current had swept thousands of giant, glowing, clear jellyfish into our midst. We found ourselves surrounded by giant, floating jellyfish. They were the size of enormous beach balls. We were right in the middle of a school of glowing jellyfish. We didn't know what to do or what to think. We just stared at each other with our mouths open in shock. It's amazing what goes through your mind in the middle of an unexpected and totally unfamiliar situation.

In that moment, I remembered a report I did in school on jellyfish. One accidental human touch could trigger them to sting. They have stinging cells on their tentacles that they use to sting or paralyze their prey before they eat them. One sting from the wrong type of jellyfish could mean death. Even though I didn't think these jellyfish were toxic, their mere size could transmit enough fluids into our bodies to possibly paralyze us forever.

I haven't gotten to the worst of it yet . . . They had gigantic bodies with long tentacles that hung from their floating bodies. The tentacles looked like real skinny, see-through, lifeless legs. The jellyfish's bodies were transparent. We could have seen right through them, except for one freaky, frightening thing . . . inside their large, transparent bodies were boys' faces. Now, that was downright spooky. In fact, it was frightening . . . not to mention totally unsettling.

The heads belonged to boys. Their blank-looking eyes were brown, and their faces were cream-colored. They just stared out into space like they were looking for something, or something was the matter. Something *was* the matter. They didn't have bodies. Just heads. Heads floating around inside of a giant, glowing, transparent jellyfish! The boys' faces didn't appear to be happy, sad, frightened, or in pain. No expression at all. Just totally blank.

My next and only thoughts were *do these jellyfish want my head next? And will I see the teenage boys who disappeared from Crossings High School?*

I was terrified. And I was ready to cry.

"Mom! Dad! Help!"

Dad was not here, so I did what I would never tell another soul I ever did in my life. I was so scared, terrified, frightened, and downright fainthearted that I peed in my pants . . . right in the ocean. Yeah. And it still didn't help because the heads didn't go away.

I immediately heard a soft voice whisper in my ear, "Jellyfish don't eat humans."

The soft whisper calmed the fear in my heart. I snapped back and thought clearly again. My mind relaxed for a moment. Suddenly I remembered . . . this was a game.

So I hollered out, "Jellyfish don't eat humans!"

At that moment, one by one, all the boys' heads disappeared from the bubble-like bodies of the jellyfish. And, just as quickly, every glowing, giant jellyfish disappeared. In their place appeared shining, colorful jellyfish the size of baseballs. They sparkled, too, like Christmas decorations. It was a wonderful sight to see. They were blue, green, purple, and even pink, but most of all, they were small. They swayed back and forth in the dark, blue ocean, gracefully opening and closing like umbrellas. Their tentacles were rhythmically swaying back and forth and opening and closing. It was an underwater ballet of jellyfish. We were captivated with the sight.

After I got my courage and swagger back, I thought to myself, *why in the world did the heads have to be boys' heads? Why couldn't they have been girls' heads?*

I know you're wondering . . . with all that going on . . . where in the world was Gabe. Well, Gabe was trying to count all the heads in each jellyfish. I don't know what he was thinking about, but when he got to number twenty-five, he got the shock of his life. He saw a head that he recognized! It was the head of his best friend. From that point on, I think he just lost it! He looked like a zombie. He had a blank look on his face. He couldn't speak. His mouth moved, but nothing came out.

When the small, multi-colored jellyfish appeared, Gabe's mind started working again. It was a strange thing. With the appearance of these fish came soft, soothing music. I don't know where it came from, but it sounded like an angelic orchestra. The music helped our nerves recover and relax from the nightmare of floating faces in the jellyfish.

"Hey, Gabe. Do you think these jellyfish sting?"

"All jellyfish sting. They don't attack humans unless you touch them. One time back at home, I stepped on one by mistake. I got stung for a minute, but it wasn't the end of the world. It did hurt, though. They're also meat eaters. That's why I freaked out when I saw my friend's head. Small jellyfish like these eat zooplanktons, other smaller fish, and sometimes other jellyfish. Bigger jellyfish eat large shrimp and other sea animals. Humans aren't sea animals. Remember… the game is based upon instincts, words, and knowledge."

Before we could get comfortable, the water started moving again. The water swirled itself around us, and it felt like we were wrapped in a cocoon. The ocean current moved swiftly, like a car speeding out of control. Instead of going straight like a car, we were being pulled down. We had been captured by the game, so to speak. When the current finally stopped, we found ourselves seated in the Abyss Zone of the ocean, 4,000 to 6,000 feet below the ocean's surface . . . in front of a school of hammerhead sharks. A school of about four hundred (you heard it right) hammerhead sharks were traveling around some undersea volcanic peaks.

The way I saw it was… we didn't have a chance to live. They say that right before a person dies, their entire life flashes before their

41

eyes. Not me. The only thing I saw was these strange-looking, huge fish with hard, hammer-shaped heads.

I didn't realize it, but the hammerhead sharks were circling around and around a fixed magnetic highway that was made from magnetic fields. If I remember correctly from Mr. Matthews' class, these fields were created by volcanic lava from centuries ago. As the sharks circled the small mountain in the middle of them, it looked like a merry-go-round. But there was nothing merry about it, at least not for us.

For a moment, I thought what we were experiencing wasn't real. Maybe it was just a fright show, or someone was really trying to scare us. But when I realized that I was only an arm's length away from a hammerhead shark's mouth, I knew then that this wasn't a show. It was real. And by the looks of the other sharks' expressions, we were either intruders or dinner . . . or both. Either way, it was not a pretty picture.

Fortunately, Gabe was running the words and the directions of the game through his head.

His mouth was moving frantically, and I could hear faintly what he was saying.

"Knowledge, instincts, and words, Knowledge, instincts, and words," he kept muttering.

I couldn't mutter or speak anything. My mind and body were frozen with fear. I was face-to-face with a hammerhead shark, and while he was studying my next move, I was studying his cold, black, icy-looking eyes that were fixed on me. He was staring like a dog, determining whether he should attack or walk away. He could sense my fear. Fear is a motivating force. When predators detect fear, they move in for the kill.

Gabe looked at me and slowly said, "Watch your words, Anton."

He was right. And I'm glad he said that because I was just about to blurt out, "Are we about to die?"

Instead, I said, "You're right, Gabe. Words, knowledge, and instinct control this game."

Gabe had also experienced mammal and reptile standoffs. Remember, he was from Brazil, and he lived in a rural town that was situated near a semi-jungle. I didn't realize it, but Gabe told me about facing deadly snakes, wildcats, and other wild animals. He had even been caught up in water currents and escaped. This was nothing new to him. Being a surfer, nothing about the ocean *seemed* to surprise him. I was with the right person.

Although Gabe and I were alike in many ways, in this moment, I realized there were some very distinct differences. He was a man from the soil, and I was a man from the cement . . . suburbs, to be exact. He really *was* from a different world. In fact, at this moment, our worlds seemed to be complete opposites.

Intelligence is based upon how well you adjust to your environment; at least, that's one definition of it. I thought Gabe's intelligence was going to get us out of this mess. These fish were looking for a meal at the bottom of the ocean, where it's dark and cold.

Gabe instinctively hollered out, "We're not part of the food chain!"

As soon as he said that, we were swept up by another ocean current and moved to warm shallow waters. We had just reacted to the situation correctly. Gabe and I were a good team. We both had the right responses. I wondered what would've happened if we had said the wrong thing.

I said out loud what I was thinking.

"I wonder what would've happened if we had said the wrong thing?"

Before I could blink, we were in front of twice as many of the same hammerhead sharks. I was beginning to realize the power of my words.

Right then and there, Gabe lost his cool, calm manners and yelled, "Reverse the game with knowledge! There's an accelerator button on the controller. Press it . . . tap it . . . faster . . . It will move us to a safe place quicker. The sharks can't out swim a game."

Frantically, I yelled, "A shark just snapped my leg. I think my skin is broken. That means blood. The smell of blood in the water means more sharks!"

"Anton, don't let your mind go. This is just a game, a *mind* game! Keep your thoughts and the controller up."

Before I knew it, we shot up like two boys playing in an elevator who had just pushed the top floor bottom.

"I got it—the controllers work with our thoughts and science knowledge, too."

I decided to push the controller one more time. It landed us on the sandy, white beach of a hot, deserted, tropical island.

I looked at Gabe and said, "Whew. Now that was a close call. I'm so glad we escaped.'

As we looked around and realized where we were, we were greatly relieved . . . and thrilled.

"Wow!! Look at where we are!" I said. "A tropical island! But, boy, am I thirsty! Wouldn't it be nice to have an ice-cold drink?"

Two glasses of ice-cold fruit punch suddenly showed up out of nowhere in our hands. At first, we were scared to drink it, and you can imagine why. Then we thought about it, looked at each other, laughed, and gulped down the cold drinks. They were totally refreshing.

"Gabe, I just thought of something. We could have finished that game in one second."

"How?"

"Jellyfish are the favorite meal of turtles. If I had remembered, I could have called forth turtles in the beginning. The jellyfish would have scattered like roaches."

Outdone by our lack of common sense, I hollered, "Somebody *slap* us!"

In a split second, an invisible hand slapped the heck out of my face.

But before it could get Gabe, he hollered, "Not me!"

So the invisible hand passed him by.

"Have you figured this game out yet?" he asked.

"I *think* Mr. Matthews' brother, Mervin, is using these games to try to force kids to think… and apply knowledge, but he's going about it in a weird way. That's why kids call him crazy. He never does anything in a 'normal' way."

Sympathizing with Mr. Matthews' brother, Gabe said, "That's not crazy."

"We were almost *killed*. It *is* crazy. If we didn't have knowledge of science, we would have died."

Then I thought about what Mervin Matthews asked us when we bought the game. He asked us if we were good students and did we know a lot about science and aquatic life. We had to have the knowledge to play this game. I had to be careful, though. I didn't want to slip and tell Gabe that we were playing a crazy and dangerous game that had been created by a crazy and dangerous teacher. And, besides, I thought we really *could* outsmart him.

Gabe was still thirsty, so he commented on it, but I don't think he was expecting a response.

"I'm still thirsty, and I wish I had another cold drink."

Out of nowhere, another unexplained, ice-cold drink popped into our hands. But this time, the drinks had a straw and a small, unexpected American flag sticking out of them. I was beginning to formulate a theory about Mervin Matthews and decided to share it with Gabe.

"You know what? I don't really think Mr. Matthews' brother is bad *or* evil. I just think he has some issues. I can just about figure out why they fired him."

Gabe was shocked.

"What!?! The video game store owner used to be a teacher. And he was fired?"

"What I *can* tell you is Mervin Matthews punished kids for not studying and learning. He had electric shocks for anyone who didn't turn in their homework or who answered a question wrong.

"Then, on the sly, he would call it an experiment. Once he overheard a student say that he hadn't taken the time to study for a test. The next day he gave the student an experiment that turned his face, arms, and hands blue for three days. When the student finally went to the hospital, the doctors couldn't figure out what was going on at all. They never did find out what made him turn blue.

"The discipline laws have changed in schools in America. Maybe Mervin Mathews was trying to take punishment back to the Dark Ages. There's no telling what he did to those kids."

Gabe dropped his head quickly.

Looking a little worried, he asked, "What kids?"

Right then and there, I changed the subject because the thought of three missing boys, truant or whatever, was too much information for my foreign friend. I didn't want to scare him, so I skipped by the subject and gave him something else to think about.

"Well, some officers from the United States Air Force escorted him off the school grounds," I said, changing the subject.

Gabe really didn't think that Mr. Matthew's brother could be that bad, given that he created a high-tech video game store for youth.

"It could just be about science," Gabe remarked, shrugging.

And once again, I said, "And why did the United States Air Force have to escort him out of the school and off the school grounds? That's serious stuff!"

I am not going to excuse Mr. Matthews' brother's behavior, and I guess Gabe finally realized that, too, because he dropped the subject and went on to a different topic.

"Anton, we've been transported to another reality! How do we get out of here?"

"Push the controller's up button."

As soon as he pushed it, we were back in the water again. But this time, our faces were out of the water, and we could see the light of day and the sunshine. Our feet and arms began to wade in the warm, blue-green ocean waters. For the first time, I actually started to feel a little safe. We could see the shore before us.

A school of dolphins was swimming toward us. They were a short distance away from us, maybe about a block away. I learned in class that dolphins are mammals, not fish, and they are friendly. However, I was still a little paranoid from our last experience. Plus, I recalled a national television news story where a caged dolphin had attacked its trainer. It didn't make sense, at least not for a dolphin. The zoo officials couldn't even rationalize the dolphin's abnormal behavior.

The dolphins were approaching us. However, they appeared to be whistling or singing. I guessed that meant they were happy. I sure hoped so.

Before I could say anything, Gabe frantically hollered, "Watch your words! Your words have power. This is a mind game. Dolphins are friendly mammals. Remember that."

CHAPTER 5

A Coincidence?

Just before we finished one episode of our spring break, another episode started. That's what I like about my life. It just keeps on going, and there are no dull days. Austin and Madison just walked through the front door. Their parents had dropped them off to work on our science project. But they didn't know our project had just moved through time and space into another dimension. It was moving just like the planets in Mr. Matthews' class.

For a moment, I wished school was open, so Gabe could see Mr. Matthews' magnificent solar system exhibit and the other exhibits on display in his classroom. I knew Gabe loved science, and Mr. Matthews' class was the place to be. It was the hotbed of the universe for all teenage science groupies.

The class science project was *nothing* compared to what Gabe and I had experienced in the ocean. It's unlikely that I could ever explain the "Aquatic Warlords" game and experience to anyone. Who would believe we had traveled outside of space and time? This wasn't a *virtual* game. It was *real*.

I just had a flashback about our Spyglass to the Skies telescope. For a moment I had forgotten the origins of Spyglass to the Skies. And now I was speculating about it. I know that a mysterious man knocked on our door and delivered a gift from yet *another* mysterious person. This gift would provide us with a tremendous amount of time to play more video games. But the video games themselves . . . were even more mystifying. Why do I feel like maybe we are being set up?

Was the telescope a gift, a means to an end, a trap, part of someone's evil plot, or were all things just working out for our good? When I look back on everything, I can't help but question the unusual things that followed its mysterious delivery: unexpected and unusual species way above the Earth and an ocean ride near the bottom of the Earth. There's no need of complaining when there are benefits at hand. Madison and Austin were really feeling the benefits of this high-end telescope. Besides, we hadn't experienced this much excitement and entertainment before.

Without question, our science project had been handed to us on a silver platter. We were ahead of the pack, and victory was at hand. Austin was so excited about all the events that had just happened that he came up with a great idea. He thought we should have special outfits for our science presentation. He always comes up with great ideas for presenting whatever we might be creating or working on together. In fact, he is pretty good at marketing.

He said, "We should stroll into class with custom-made T-shirts that read 'Science, the New Cool'. Maybe we could get extra credit if we use that as our theme. 'Science, the New Cool'. It might even start a science movement at our entire school and then spread throughout the country. You never know."

"That's big thinking," I said.

"Think about it. We could get lots of credit."

He had more than a good idea; he had a case, as always. To support his theme, "Science, the New Cool," he came up with lots of reasons why science was cool, and Gabe, the whiz kid, added more.

The arrival of the new-found telescope was really making me think about a lot of things. One of them, of course, was our science project. We had decided to call our project "Planet Journeys." Hey!!! Wait a minute! We had named our science project "Planet Journeys"; then, I received a mysterious, professional telescope from an unknown person; and, finally, we purchased video games that took us into another galactic dimension.

Also, right when we were exiting the class before the break, Mr. Matthews came up to us and said, "I'm depending on you to do well on this project."

Words are powerful, and they have life and energy. Words can make you feel good about yourself, better about yourself, or they can make you feel horrible and bad about who you are. Mr. Matthews' words to us made us feel like we really wanted to make our project spectacular.

The new telescope was just the thing that we needed to make our project fantastic. It had so many cool parts and pieces and programs and software that we kept discovering. One of the things that we found was a mechanism to take live pictures. That means if we photograph the planets, the moon, and the stars up close, we could create a very slick presentation. We could create a project that would be unforgettable and the talk of the school. Imagine that!

Technology is cool beyond words. It has a way of pushing you up higher and faster.

The more we talked about the telescope and the games and the weird circumstances behind how they came into our hands in the first place, the more we were beginning to think that maybe... just *maybe*... there was some kind of connection between Mervin Matthews, his top-level science secrets, the video games, and the telescope.

There was also another realization that was slowly beginning to dawn on all of us. We were beginning to realize that we might be entering into a realm or dimension that would take us farther than we planned to go . . . and keep us longer than we had ever planned to stay.

CHAPTER 6

Instincts and Knowledge

Gabe was over the top with excitement.

With a rushing enthusiasm, he said, "Let's start the next game!"

Austin and Madison didn't know what had occurred with our first video game, "Aquatic Warlords," so they were a little surprised at my response.

"*That* wasn't a game," I said. "It was a *very* unusual field trip, a dangerous episode! In fact, while we were playing the game, I had the eerie feeling that there was someone watching us all the time. The game was being regulated."

Gabe was still sympathizing with Mervin Matthews.

"I think that Mervin Matthews was just trying to teach us a lesson," he said.

Gabe just didn't get it. He didn't know or understand that Mr. Matthew's brother was over the edge and somewhat psycho. In the best way I could, I tried to explain my take on the situation.

"Listen, Gabe," I explained. "I don't think the game was just based upon our words, instinct, and scientific knowledge. I think there was something else taking place, like maybe a control room behind the scenes, where everything was being secretly controlled by someone or something we couldn't see."

For a second, Gabe's mouth dropped open.

When he was finally able to speak, he finally said, "Huh? A control room? What's a control room?"

"It's the kind of control room that NASA uses when they watch a spaceship launch into orbit from Earth. The control room monitors the spacecraft and the astronauts. They also stand ready to help if the spacecraft and its crew get in any danger."

Gabe was quiet and somewhat puzzled.

Then he said, "So we weren't alone when we were playing the game?"

"Probably not," I said.

Austin interjected, "Didn't you say that Mr. Matthews' brother worked at NASA once? If he did, he would know about send-offs and control rooms."

From my standpoint, it all appeared like a plot. I couldn't help but say the obvious.

"He probably was the one I sensed watching us."

As Madison and Austin were listening to Gabe and I discuss Mervin Matthews' game, they were trying to fill in the blanks. But they really didn't have a full picture of what we were talking about because we still hadn't told them what had happened. It's hard to explain to someone or anyone that the games take place in another dimension. That's because we don't understand the dimension ourselves. Perhaps we should say that we were shot like a missile into another reality, another world, just like a rocket launches a satellite into orbit.

We weren't even going to *try* to explain the mysterious human figure we had seen. Maybe we should do the same thing with the video games that we did with the telescope and just wait for their responses and reactions. However, there's just one other real factor to consider… the games were dangerous. The mysterious teenage girl was not.

In the meantime, Gabe was getting persistent about playing the games. He was eager to start the next one. His next response confirmed to me that he was a little naïve and still trusting Mr. Matthews' brother too much.

"I think the next game is safe," he said. "Look. The games are based on knowledge, words, and instincts. We can assume the rules won't change. We can also assume we'll know most of the answers to the 'Solar System Stretch' game."

Gabe is pretty smart, but he was beginning to sound like a sucker. I wasn't afraid of the games, but I understood the real risks of them. "Solar System Stretch" wasn't a normal game. It was my responsibility to get everyone to start thinking wisely, so I took charge.

"What happens if we're on real planets? Four of our solar system's planets are rocky: Mercury, Venus, Mars, and Earth. The other four planets are composed of gases and liquids. You can't even stand on the surface of Jupiter, Saturn, Uranus, or Neptune. So where does that leave us?

"Mercury and Venus are next to the sun and hot . . . hot, to be exact. By the time we figure out the right response or right words, we could be toasted. Neptune is a dark refrigerator. There's no telling what the game might ask us about Neptune. If we saw live boys' heads inside giant jellyfish in 'Aquatic Warlords,' we just might end up seeing the abominable snowman on Neptune. It's going to be something crazy . . . trust me."

After I said we saw live boys' heads in a choir-like fashion inside the bellies of giant jellyfish, Madison, and Austin almost fainted.

They were both astonished, and they both shouted, "Whaaat!?!"

Gabe trusted me, but it was clear that he also trusted Mr. Matthews' brother quite a bit. I guess that would be easy to understand since Gabe had never met Mervin Matthews and knew very little about him.

"Mr. Matthew's brother didn't create these games to kill kids. He will help us if we get in trouble. I think that's the reason for the control room. If we need to get out, the controller will help us just like it did before . . . and, of course, our words, knowledge, and instincts."

"Do we even know enough science to play the game, or are we riding completely on our instincts?" Madison asked. "I am not into dying early. I am a kid. I got a whole life ahead of me.

57

"Besides, we still don't know why those guys from the United States Air Force escorted Mr. Matthews' brother out of the school. The principal could have called the police or a local sheriff. Why did he have to call *them*?"

Like me, Madison recalled the incident. It's hard not to. "It's not game time," Austin said. "It's study time. We need to find out what the crazy former science teacher is thinking."

Then he came up with a really good idea.

"We can study the solar system through the telescope's 'Instructions and Guide to the Planets' book before we play the 'Solar System Stretch' game."

"That's a good point," I said.

And it was. Austin was always good at coming up with strategies.

He wasn't hesitating about playing the games at all. Remember, he was with me when I purchased them, so he was *expecting* to play the games. Although he hadn't studied the directions, he felt like he was up for the games. He had no idea what he was getting into; neither did I. I just hoped with his gaming knowledge, he would be able to get us out.

I see myself as a leader, so I had to stand up and take the lead.

"We can't outsmart Mervin Matthews," I said, "but we can sure outplay him in the games."

We were a winning team: me, Austin, and Madison. We were some of the top gamers at Crossings. And with quick-on-his-feet

Gabe on our team, we had a fighting chance. Four minds were sure better than one. We had four days left in spring break. If we were going to play the games, we needed to get started right away . . . since there were two parts to the game.

Everyone wasn't ready to play the final play.

"Now, who is Mr. Matthews' brother again?" Madison asked.

"Mervin Matthews. He was Crossings' physics teacher, who did a summer internship and worked at NASA," I answered.

"I don't remember him."

"That's because he was the physics teacher, and we don't take physics."

Madison was very curious about Mervin Matthews.

"I would like to go to the game store and pay Mr. Matthews' brother a visit. I wonder what would happen if we all went together to see him? I bet he would be surprised. Let's go tomorrow and ask him a few questions about the games and his motives, especially since we just have four days to play the games and finish our science class project."

Austin responded quickly.

"Not me. I have to go somewhere with my parents, so I only have three days left. Let's skip the games shop. We have the instructions here."

Madison and Austin didn't know what they were in for. I thought they should at least be warned, so I honestly told them what I thought.

"After playing the last game," I said, "I am certain that Mervin Matthews has more than just playing games on his mind. I believe the guy has some kind of hidden agenda. He's either trying to force kids to learn, use what they have learned, or kill them. Learning science isn't a life and death matter."

"Anton might have a good point," Gabe said. "Adults shaped the world we live in now. Maybe he thinks we are going to mess up civilization. He's got a point."

Madison, Austin, and I kept bouncing back and forth about what we thought Mervin Matthews' philosophies on life and science were.

Gabe finally said, "Science runs things."

"No. People run things," Austin responded.

Madison is always trying to be fair and a peacemaker.

So she ended the debate on Mervin Matthews' philosophies by saying, "Everyone has a place in society. Science makes life interesting and fun."

"Maybe Mr. Matthews' brother is just scared," Gabe said.

"Scared of what? He didn't look scared to me," I said.

What I really wanted to tell Gabe was that every once in a while, there is a bad teacher in the bunch… just like a bad apple. Coming from Brazil, Gabe may not have understood that. Besides, I didn't want him to go back to Brazil saying that American teachers were bad. That would ruin the reputations of really good teachers like Mr. Matthews. So I stopped trying to prove my point about bad teachers, although everyone knows they exist.

Madison was impatient and insisted.

"I just want to go to the game store before I play this game. I want to ask some questions and get a feel for this guy. After all, he's Mr. Matthews' brother. He can't be all that bad."

I didn't want to sound like the bad guy, but I had to keep reminding everyone who this guy was.

The four of us had started reviewing the directions and instructions from Mervin Matthews' final game, "Solar System Stretch." After reading the directions, Madison announced that she still thought we should go to the game store and pay Mervin Matthews a visit. She wanted firm answers to a few questions that weren't in the game's directions. So we all headed to the game store.

The lines outside the store continued to be backed up. Teenagers, kids, and parents were in line to get into the store.

Austin looked at the line outside the store and said, "Do we really need to talk to him before we play the game? This line is awfully long. We'll be here all day trying to get in."

"No, we won't," Madison said. "I have a lifetime family club pass, so we don't have to wait in line."

"How did *you* get a family club card if you've never been here?" I said.

Madison confidently replied, "My uncle was the architect that designed this building. He didn't have any kids, so he gave the pass to our family."

Madison held the card up real high like a flag so that everyone, I mean everyone, could see it.

Then she said, "Just keep walking. Walk straight to the door."

The security guard looked at the four of us.

"Stop. Where's your pass?" he asked.

Madison stopped, turned around, looked up at him, and held up the pass. The security guard looked at us in unbelief, but he was stuck, and he knew it. He had to let us through the line and into the store. We walked into the store very quickly before the security guard could think of any more questions. We all high-fived each other and laughed. I really wasn't sure if the security guard would let us in.

Once we got in the store and moved farther away from the entrance door, Madison looked at us and jokingly said, "I used the family pass, and we *are* family. We're a family of pro gamers."

Austin and I were familiar with Mervin. Matthews' game store, but Gabe wasn't. This was his first time at the store. When he looked around and saw the thousands of video games from all over the world, he lost it. I don't mean he had a nervous breakdown. He didn't start laughing. He just got real quiet. He kept looking around and around. He acted like a five-year-old child that had gotten twice as many toys as he had expected on his birthday. His eyes were enormous as he looked around the store, trying to take everything in at once. Needless to say, the game store had made a great impression on Gabe.

We expected him to snap out of this ecstatic state real soon. But it didn't happen. Gabe is a teenager, but he continued to act like a kid on Christmas morning, going from toy to toy. Instead of toys, he went from section to section of the game store, from Spanish, Japanese, Chinese, and even European games . . . and on and on. After he had wandered through most areas of the store, he walked back toward us in amazement.

"Life is large in America!" he remarked. "These games are out of this world! If we don't do anything but play video games my entire spring break vacation, it's ok by me. There is a lot for me to learn here."

One of Mervin Matthews' employees, dressed in a black turtleneck and straight-legged black pants, walked up to us and asked, "May I help you?"

A moment later, another spy-looking guy in the same designer, black turtleneck and straight-legged, black pants walked up to Austin and asked, "Are you all a team, or do you need some help, too?"

Gabe turned his head toward me and quietly spoke in Spanish.

"These clerks look like Batman and Robin in black."

Then he laughed out loud. He had a point. They did look like characters out of a movie. And I laughed, too.

The male clerks acted like they didn't hear him.

The first clerk said, "What was that?"

The second clerk disappeared quickly and came back with two games. He handed the games to us. One game was titled "Batman and Robin". The second game was the cartoon, "Sponge Bob." Apparently, they had understood Gabe and clearly understood Spanish.

The joke was on us. Both men looked at us and laughed and laughed. For a moment, we were kind of embarrassed. There was no need of feeling guilty. What had just happened *was* funny, so we laughed at ourselves, too. Our laughter broke the ice with them. Once we stopped laughing, the store clerk asked us a question in a friendly and respectful manner.

"Do you need help?"

Madison spoke up for the group.

"Yes, we're here for the games of the future.

The store clerk pointed towards the "Games of the Future" room and said, "That way."

Mervin Matthews was standing at command when we entered the "Games of the Future" room. He looked like he was surprised to see us back so soon. It had only been a few days since our first visit.

In addition to his normal black outfit, he had a small red, white, and blue flag pin on his uniform. I wondered what that was about. It seemed out of character. But who knows what to expect from a man rumored to have high-level government secrets. I guess he was wearing the flag pin to make believe he was still at NASA. Or perhaps, he wanted to act like he was functioning in the best interest of our country. But it was obvious he was still trying to hide something. I bet he is on the government's surveillance watch list.

We were here for answers and directions, not observations. Madison still had some questions that she wanted to ask him about the "Solar System Stretch" game. Madison was usually pretty good with people, and they tend to take to her very quickly. But she was about to get a runaround with Mervin Matthews. She kept on asking questions that he wouldn't answer. Like... what's the real objective of this game? Is the game restricted to the solar system? Does the game have anything to do with the United States Space Station?

His response to every question was simply, "You'll learn as you go."

It was plain to see. The man was set on making us play "the game" his way.

"I don't get it," Madison said.

"You will," he responded. "I can see you are inquisitive, but does that translate into grades?"

Madison just looked at him like he was ridiculous and silly. He had avoided every one of her questions. Then he turned the focus entirely on her and played a game of child psychology. He started evaluating her behavior instead of his own behavior.

Next, it was my turn to ask questions, and I wasn't going to fail.

"Do you have a twin brother?" I asked him.

His expression changed. He looked directly at me and frowned. To me, his frown was telling me that I was intruding. It also said back off. However, after a moment, he surprised me. He changed his facial expression and spoke with a warm smile on his face.

"I am from a big family with lots of brothers, and we all look alike."

At that moment, I felt like I might have jumped to conclusions and misread him. Maybe there was a strand of kindness and humanity within him. His face lit up when he talked about his brothers. His facial expressions demonstrated that he cared about somebody. That's a start. Maybe I should give him the benefit of the doubt.

I don't know any other adult who would spend thousands and thousands of dollars on a game store for kids. I didn't know all of his motives . . . but maybe they couldn't be all that bad. It just seemed like he didn't like answering questions.

CHAPTER 7

Reddish-Orange Planet

Madison thought she needed her questions answered in order to play the game successfully. Gabe and I had played one part of the game already, so we knew that courage, knowledge, and mad-like instincts were how you played it. The rules said knowledge, instincts, and words. But, as we discovered, courage should have been added first.

This game was not like any high school quiz or test we had ever taken. In fact, it wasn't like *any* kind of test or quiz. Knowing the answers to the questions was not enough. For these games, you had to be quick on your feet and in survival mode at all times. The game was exhilarating and, at the same time, scary as hell. And it didn't hurt to be smart. Smart and courageous were important keys to be added to knowledge, instincts, and words.

Even knowing everything that we knew, there was still no way that Gabe and I could prepare Madison and Austin for the games, especially the "Solar System Stretch" game. In fact, we didn't realize just how unprepared *we* were to play part one of the game. If we did, we would have stopped before we started and sought more directions.

We started the "Solar System Stretch" game from the basement in my house. This game was different from "Aquatic Warlords"; however, there was one similarity. Both games required wrist controllers to start. Once we pressed the controllers, the difference between the two games became apparent.

Each one of us had a wrist controller attached to our arms and one by one, we pressed them. Instead of tumbling through a glowing, tunnel-like portal, the game propelled us, one by one, through a brilliant, white, round, spinning-door portal. In one motion, we exited Earth's atmosphere. The "Solar System Stretch" game had started. Time stopped for one whole minute… then it happened.

With a startled look on her face. Madison turned directly to me.

"This is NOT Earth! This is NOT a virtual reality game. We're in another dimension! So, what's next?"

I would have taken a long pause before replying to her question, but I didn't have time. So, I gave her a quick answer.

"Gabe and I played the first game, 'Aquatic Warlords'. The controllers got us in the game. In the last game, there were different tests and trials. Once we passed one test, we went on to the next one."

Then I whispered, "If you don't pass . . . I guess you are in danger."

Before I could finish my last sentence, Austin cut in and asked, "You get stuck in the game, huh?"

I shook my head and said, "Not certain, but it could be something like that. We didn't cross that road. This is another game, a new one. The store clerk just told us to watch our words, don't be scared . . . and *think* before we speak. I believe . . . we are the first ones to play this game."

We were out of time for questions . . . because, as far as I could see . . . there were raging, fierce, non-stop winds circling the place where we had just arrived. The course, reddish-orange sand we were standing on whirled with the winds. The rocky landscape was reddish-orange, too. We were standing in the middle of a real-life, raging sandstorm. We had entered into the unexpected. There was no snooze button. We were well on our way for a rude and rough awakening. In fact, we were standing there in a state of shock. And this was real.

I could only imagine one place in the whole solar system that fits the description of this place, where I was now standing with my three friends. By the looks of things, we had arrived on the planet Mars. The reddish-orange, deep valleys, and the reddish-orange, vast mountains confirmed everything I had ever learned in science class about Mars. There was only one place where the rusty iron turned the dust and the entire planet reddish-orange . . . Mars! The rusty iron also turned the Earth's Grand Canyon a reddish-orange, but this wasn't Earth.

To be honest, I wasn't really sure if we were on Mars. I remembered, again from science class, how difficult it was to land on Mars. So, I had second thoughts about our landing. *What's the chance of high school kids landing on Mars, anyway?*

No descent. No touchdown. We were just there.

Mr. Mathews had taught us that Mars was the most difficult planet to land on because of its thin atmosphere. The atmospheric pressure is low, less than 1% of the Earth's surface pressure. If a spacecraft tries to land on Mars, it would fall quickly or crash suddenly because of the thin atmosphere.

For years countries have made unsuccessful attempts at landing humans on Mars. NASA had problems landing on Mars, too. It's the destination of choice for all space agencies. And we just showed up …and made it to the finish line. We should have been ecstatic about making it to the finish line, but we weren't because we didn't know what was next on this side of the galaxy.

Well, it didn't take us long to accept our new reality. In fact, we snapped out of our state of shock quickly because we realized, real fast, that we were in survival mode. Trust me; this didn't feel like a game.

The wind was so fierce that we could barely hear each other. I reminded my friends, once again, that we were in a game that was based upon and played with three main rules:

K n o w l e d g e * I n s t i n c t s * W o r d s.

Knowledge said we were on Mars. Instinct said we wouldn't last long in the midst of these hurricane-like winds.

I didn't expect it to be warm on Mars because, as a rule, it's not warm there. We needed to be close to the equator since the equator region is the only warm place on the planet. The majority of the planet is colder than Antarctica, with temperatures cold enough to turn humans into lifeless, frozen statues. In contrast, during the summer season Mars' temperatures at the equator can reach as high as 70 degrees Fahrenheit at noon, but the nighttime temperatures are deadly cold like the rest of the planet. During the night, temperatures can plunge to minus 100 degrees Fahrenheit. Knowing all this, we had to figure out a way to get the heck out of Mars before night.

We discovered that it might have been easier to *arrive* on this planet than to *leave* it. I had just recalled that the game was time sensitive. Knowing that we were going to be forced to remember everything we had learned and heard about Mars . . . just to survive.

From the corner of my eye to my far right, I noticed there were some enormous and some smaller reddish-orange mountains a distance away. The image of mountains spelled shelter and relief from the fast and furious dust storm that pressed against our bodies and etched across our faces. Here the wind and dust went hand and hand.

"Let's head toward those mountains over there!" I yelled, pointing toward the mountains.

We pressed toward the mountains with our eyes almost shut to avoid the raging dust particles brushing against our eyelids. It's not generally a good idea to walk with your eyes practically shut. However, because the ground before us was flat and dry, with the exception of a few small craters, walking wasn't too risky.

We walked as fast as we could, given the circumstances. The walking wasn't as fast as we would have liked because the unyielding, howling winds were exhausting us. Plus, our resistance was just about gone. We tried to keep walking as the swirling, hurricane-force winds almost swept us off the ground. The mountains were only a stretch away. The distance didn't matter anymore because we had physically reached our end. We couldn't reach the mountains or overcome the wind.

There was only one thing left. It was time to use the third rule of the game, our words. Our words had power. We needed a loophole in this game to stop the madness, and we had it. I have never read anywhere that says Mars' hurricane-like winds are 24/7. Therefore, it was time to use our words . . . and call things that "be not" as though "they were".

Out of my mouth, I hollered, "Winds! Be still!"

And the winds calmed down and stopped. Madison and Austin stood looking at me with their mouths wide open and their eyes bulging. This game was new to them, and seeing the power of words at work threw them for a loop. And it showed on their faces. They looked at me as if I had performed some kind of miracle. The grin on Gabe's face said he was all in. It was obvious he was loving it.

He regained his swag and confidence and hollered, "Let the games begin! We're masters!"

We had conquered the first part of the game, but the second part was about to meet us soon.

We finally reached the mountains. The winds had disappeared. What a relief! On the left end of the first set of mountains, we noticed a small opening that led to a cave. Since the wind was no longer challenging us, we were able to think, and we thought about exploring signs of past or even present life inside the small cave.

The cave gave us a chance to do something other than just survive. We were able to take a brief rest from the challenging weather conditions. Daylight was still stretching over the vast Mars sky. We thought we had enough time to explore the cave. Cautiously we entered the cave. To our surprise, the cave's walls were damp. A wet cave near the equator was a good place to search for life.

We weren't expecting life on Mars to look like life on Earth. After all, through the telescope, we had viewed what appeared to be a *blue*, dancing teenage girl dashing like a deer in and out of the mountains on Mars. Even if she was an imagination, there was still a strand of reality to her image, at least for us.

As we walked through the cave that was sprinkled with rays of light, Madison asked a very good question.

"Do you think we are alone here?"

We didn't have an answer, but the situation spoke for itself. There were no unfamiliar voices or sounds echoing in the cave. Although the cave didn't seem to have any sign of life, we thought there might be life underneath the planet's surface. So, we decided to leave the cave.

Right before we turned around to leave, from a distance deep along the caves' walls, we noticed lights sparkling like falling snowflakes. It was the same marvelous light we witnessed in the spinning portals that transported us here. Something about the light felt comfortable, so we continued to walk in the direction of the sparkling blanket of lights.

As we moved closer to the lights, we noticed something rather odd.

"The lights are moving away from us," Austin said. "This is the second turn we have made toward them. As we move closer to them, they move farther away from us, as if they were motioning us to follow them."

He was right. The bright snowflake-like bundle of lights inside the dark cave was moving us farther into the dark cave. Finally, the lights stopped moving. The question was why. Then we found the answer. The answer wasn't before us. It was below our bodies, right underneath our feet. There it was . . . something we never thought we would ever see on Mars, a narrow stream of crystal-clear water with majestic, purple, flower-shaped images swaying back and forth in the water like moving watercolors. The stream wasn't real large, maybe the size of a closet door. The water was flowing from another part of the cave that we couldn't see because of the hollow darkness.

With the exception of the howling wind, the swiping sand, and hundreds of sparkling, white, light particles that guided us to the foot of the stream, this was the first movement of any kind that we witnessed from any living thing.

"Swish, swish!"

Right before our eyes, the water's bright, airy, flowery matter whirled around like an array of rainbow colors. It looked like a beautiful performance of colors and flowers and crystal-clear water. Then suddenly, splashes of water rushed upon our feet and clothes from the stream. We couldn't help but wonder if it, or they were trying to communicate with us. Their lively water performance seemed more of a welcome than a warning.

There was more to come. The purple images transformed into words right before our eyes. Then, ever so slowly, the words formed into a sentence. The sentence floated in midair.

The sentence read: *The Top. Go to The Top.*

"What does that mean? And why are the words in English?" Madison asked.

"Maybe that's the way we are seeing them. We are seeing them through English eyes," Austin replied.

We waited anxiously for more words. But they didn't come. Then the water stopped splashing, and the stream returned back to normal. The stream's images vanished, too.

"What's 'The Top'? The top of what? That wasn't enough information. Maybe it's something to come," Gabe remarked.

"I don't know," Austin said, "but we just followed a bunch of lights deeper into this dark cave. We need to get out of here before the lights go out."

Madison, Gabe, and I stood around for a while, waiting for something else to occur. Not Austin. He analyzed the situation real fast, turned around, and started walking toward the entrance of the cave. He didn't look back.

After a few minutes, Madison shouted, "Wait, Austin!"

Then she ran and caught up with him. Her voice echoed throughout the cave.

Gabe and I were still marveling about the aquatic performance and the mysterious messages and hoping at any moment there would be more. Our hope wasn't enough to hold our attention, especially since we knew our time on Mars was limited.

Gabe looked at me, somewhat disappointed, and said, "It's up to the real astronauts to explore life on Mars, not us."

So, we left.

Outside the cave, Austin glanced at us and then looked around at the planet and said, "So what are we supposed to do next?"

"Just wait and see," I said. "There's a sequence of reactions that follows every action."

No sooner had I finished my sentence then the game made a big shift. We shifted from the mountain terrains to the massive canyons of Mars. There is something special and spectacular about the massive canyons. The very sight of them was overwhelming and overpowering. We again stood in awe, mouths hanging open, unable to speak. From the West to the East. From the North to the South. And to the very bottom. There was no end in sight of the massive canyons.

With a sense of certainty and awe, Gabe said, "This is breathtaking! I know now where we are. These are the Grand Canyons of Mars, Valles Marineris. They're the largest canyons on Mars and the largest canyons in the entire galaxy. I learned about them in school."

"Wait! Did anyone notice we were just moved around like puppets?" Austin asked.

Still in amazement at the canyons, Gabe replied "It's a game we agreed to play. Let's just enjoy it while we are here and finish the game."

"Hold it!" Austin said. "We are falling through tunnels and portals, and we don't know what time it is. What's the purpose of this game?"

I had to get Austin refocused.

"Well, we can't go back, Austin," I said. "So, let's just move forward together. The game said we do have some control by our knowledge, instincts, and words."

He decided to calm down and go with the flow. We walked as close as we could to the edge of the canyons and veered down at the bottomless, sculptured pits. From what we could see, there didn't appear to be any life there. No rivers, streams, or trees. Not even dried bushes.

The canyons looked like upside-down mountains. I, for one, had never witnessed anything this vast before. We probably looked like nothing but tiny little dots in the middle of these enormous canyons.

Gabe had walked way ahead of us. I think he was trying to capture in his mind everything he saw. It was like he was trying to take photos in his mind. It didn't matter how fast he walked; that wasn't going to happen. He needed a plane and an extra day, and he didn't have either.

Valles Marineris canyons caught our attention along with some other things. It didn't take long for us to notice that the mountains weren't the only thing that had shifted. The weather was changing, too. The temperature was dropping rapidly. The cold temperature signaled that we were farther away from the equator and the night was approaching. It was cold, too cold for us to remain on Mars, and the temperature continued to drop by the minute. Time was also against us now. The last thing we needed was a delay, but that was just what we got!

Suddenly, out of nowhere and as far as we could see, there were reddish-orange, ancient-looking dwarfs coming up from out of the canyons. They were coming from every direction. They marched two-by-two in long, sweeping lines that spread across the canyons. They looked like soldiers… or robots. We didn't know if they were coming to meet us or if their destination was directing them our way. I don't normally think of dwarfs as violent, but this was Mars, not Earth. If they were violent, we sure needed to have a strategy or a game plan.

Everyone looked at Austin for an answer. His eyes looked back at us with that I-told-you-so expression. Strangely enough, my mind rolled back into gear, and I calmly reminded everyone of the strategies we had in our arsenal.

"Come on, you guys. Remember that knowledge, instincts, and our words are our weapons. They worked once, so they'll work again."

That was just a pretty bold thing for me to say. The truth is that, like everybody else, I was scared.

In full force, the dwarfs approached us, marching steadily, with no break in their stride or rhythm. It wouldn't be long before we met their fearless leader. I assumed there was one. As they marched toward us, they looked like rows of robots. Their arms and legs moved in perfect motion. It was almost as if they were marching to the beat of an invisible drum that only they could hear.

Then they started to chant with rhythm. It wasn't a song; it was a chant. As they advanced closer to us, the volume of the chant increased. The marching seemed more deliberate, and they had stern looks on their faces. It was a little bit unsettling, this army of dwarfs marching in unison and chanting as they marched. It didn't make sense to run, especially since they would probably catch up with us anyway. Besides, we didn't have time.

No one had to say a word. I sensed what was running through everyone's mind. *Why would you buy a game that would get us stuck on Mars for life?* I even thought that NASA might want to reconsider racing to Mars. I asked myself why we came to Mars in the first place. Was it because of the dancing girl who was so full of joy? I wasn't experiencing joy right now. Where was the singing girl when we needed her? We were nervous for our lives, and our thoughts were racing and crashing!

Then out of nowhere, the happy, airy-looking girl appeared. She didn't come too close to us, but she was close enough for us to "feel" her presence. She released waves of her presence, and they filled the atmosphere like sound waves. I hadn't felt anything like this before.

"You know what, Madison?" I said. "There is something pretty special about this girl. I feel like we could be friends with her forever."

Madison just nodded.

"I felt that way from the first time I spotted her through the telescope," she said.

Upon the happy, airy girl's arrival, the dwarfs suddenly changed their chant to an upbeat "Danc, danc, danc" and began to dance. They moved their legs and feet up and down swiftly and swung their hips and arms like clock-work from side to side. I couldn't interpret their words, but the tone of the chant had changed. It felt more inviting. The expression in their eyes changed, too.

At first, their eyes were a cold, dark brown. In contrast to their cold, mean, dark eyes, now the dwarfs' eyes were glimmering with a bluish-white glow like that of the dancing girl. Their eyes seemed full of joy. Within moments of their eyes changing, the dancing girl vanished before our eyes.

Austin said suddenly, "Hey! I don't feel cold anymore. I wonder what happened."

"It's a game," I said. "Once you begin to conquer the game…the elements change. In our case, the elements were wind, temperature,

81

and fear. When you conquer one element, like fear, all the other elements drop off automatically."

Still explaining the game, I said, "Mars was game one. Now that we finished it, it's time to leave. We've quenched our desire to find life on Mars. The game is called "Solar System Stretch." That means there's more than one planet in this game."

"Do we get to pick the next planet?" Madison asked.

"No," I replied. "The game picks the next destination."

CHAPTER 8

Human Satellites

No amount of studying could have prepared us for the next part of the game.

The way these games were designed and how they were played made me more sure than ever that Mervin Matthews worked for NASA. His thoughts, plans, and pursuits were totally disconnected from the world we knew and were familiar with. He *couldn't* have stayed at Crossings High School because he didn't belong there. He just didn't fit!

Now I was beginning to comprehend why four Air Force officers escorted him from the school. Based on what he had done in the past to students who didn't "come up to his standards", so to speak, the principal understood that he possibly needed to keep an eye on Mervin Matthews, maybe even remove him as a teacher. Mervin Matthews was capable of doing something exceedingly far beyond anything that a normal person could think, imagine, or do.

Knowing what he knew about Mervin Matthews, the principal (and all of us students, for that matter) didn't know what he might do next. One thing the principal was sure of, though. Mervin Matthews had to go. He had to be removed . . . by any means necessary. And because of his supposed connection with NASA, it seemed that an official committee from the military would be the best approach. He just didn't belong at Crossings High. And we didn't belong where we had just been deposited . . . billions of miles from Earth.

It would have been best for us to close our eyes during the next episode of the game and just pretend like we didn't exist. That sounds like dying, doesn't it? Well, we were close to it.

There are times in life when it's not necessary to see and know everything that's going on. For instance… all four of us were actually suspended in the air like an airplane in the middle of Neptune's gas and liquid surface along with its deadly poisonous atmosphere.

We learned that Neptune was not made for human beings, nor animals or plants for that matter. There is no life on Neptune; there's a reason why. The place is abnormally cold and freezing. To make matters worse, Neptune's surface is made of cold, deadly gases and liquids. You can't place your foot on the ground because there is no ground! It's just liquid and gas. Perhaps that's why the four of us were spinning around and around Neptune's atmosphere like a satellite. We weren't in a spacecraft or a ship. We were outside like birds on a string.

This wasn't our idea of space travel, nor our idea of a new thrilling video game. We all knew whose idea this was. We did not have to mention his name again; it wasn't necessary.

Our predicament reminded me of the time I went to Six Flags as a kid and rode the airplane ride. Airplane rides go around and around, and then the ride speeds up and goes so fast that the little kids start screaming. Some even vomit. Well, that was us. But we were so cold that our tongues were almost stuck to our mouths and lips.

We didn't have seat belts. Our bodies remained flying like birds together; like birds without wings, we were unable to break away from Neptune's magnetic pull.

We were circling Neptune like the Moon circles the Earth. I have to tell you what our eyes were staring directly down at . . . let me describe it to you. We were hanging over the planet like vapors of smoke, which hang over an open pot of hot soup or chili. Instead of the pot being hot, it happened to be cold. The dangerous fumes from Neptune's gases came up into our nostrils. We could hardly breathe. In fact, we were afraid *to* breathe because of the poisonous vapors. This was criminal.

Madison whispered to me that she was about to faint.

I warned her, "If you do, we will never see you again."

Gabe just straight out told her, "Shut up and watch your words, Madison! Remember. In this game, your words have power, and whatever you say happens."

With that said, I was trying to really figure out what to say and how to get us out of this game with my words.

Based on our past adventures together, Austin was normally the one who got us out of jams. He was known as the "Strategy Guy." Whenever there was a problem that the three of us were confronted with, we would call on him.

"Hey, "Strategy Guy". Fix this!" we would say.

Austin will probably most likely succeed as a business executive someday because business executives solve big problems and help organizations run better. And that's what he's good at.

At this moment, however, frost was hanging from Austin's eye-lashes, and his short, curly hair was topped with frost. His hair looked like the frost on the grass during the first real cold day of winter. For a moment, I thought Austin's brain was freezing, too, because he wasn't responsive to anything. It was obvious he couldn't handle the freezing temperatures of Neptune.

The temperatures were so cold that blood wasn't running to our brains too fast, either. It sure seemed like it because we were all just hanging in midair with our teeth chattering, covered with frost, and saying nothing . . . actually *unable* to say a single word.

Neptune's cold winds were violent and in constant motion. Its mighty winds were ten times greater than those on Mars. The winds were swirling around at high speeds, ten times faster than Earth's worst hurricanes. In fact, Neptune's hurricane winds were the most violent winds in the solar system. They were so strong and violent that they continuously changed the planet's surface.

This wasn't a game any longer, and it *certainly* wasn't a field trip . . . it was a death trap.

Gabe was totally silent, too, as a result of the frigid temperature. Remember, he was from Brazil. So, you can imagine the effects of the frigid cold on him! Poor guy. What a vacation for him!! He had gone into a zombie-like state again. This must have been some kind of survival mechanism for him. Remember, he did the same thing when we encountered the giant jellyfish with his best friend's head in it. Now, Gabe's mind is so fast that he probably assessed the entire situation that we were in and shut down before he froze to death. At least he was still with us.

Man! If we could just get a little heat, we could get more blood flowing to our brains. That would give us more power to think better. We needed to think our way out of this situation. And since we were all too frozen to speak, thinking was our only hope at this moment. We *did* have answers and knowledge. It's that our minds just weren't working . . . it was too cold. That's why there was no life on this planet. It was too shivering cold!

So, here we were. Suspended in the air. Unable to control our direction or course. Floating around and around above the planet. Unable to speak, move, or think. We were Neptune's human satellites.

Gabe's frigid body started to sink down toward Neptune's surface. I was concerned about him, but in that moment, I was also concerned about what and how I was going to explain to my father that I had lost my friend and house guest. As he descended, getting closer and closer to the cold, dark, poisonous gases, they became thicker and deadlier. Our Brazilian friend was about to die right in our midst. We stared down at him . . . helpless and hopeless. And he looked up toward us with an expression of helplessness and hopelessness.

I became very angry at our predicament and our inability to do anything to help our friend. I started shaking and twisting, trying to free myself from the grips of the freezing temperatures . . . and the magnetic pull. I guess my anger generated some heat in me, and I was able to shake something loose in me, along with some of the cold.

I was able to speak, even though it was a little faint at first.

I whispered, "If we could just get a little heat for our bodies to warm up, this would send oxygen to our brains."

Madison and Austin looked at me with puzzled expressions. They knew I had said something, but they couldn't understand it.

My frustration and anger together allowed me to scream, "IF WE COULD GET SOME HEAT, IT WOULD WARM UP OUR BODIES AND GET SOME OXYGEN TO OUR BRAINS!!"

By that time, Gabe had sunk down so low that he was just about to drop into the poisonous gas. However, as soon as I hollered out those words, the blue, dancing, singing girl appeared. I thought she was from Mars, but it was now clear . . . she belonged to the universe! She was a helper, a strengthener, and a stand-by for us in the time of trouble.

Her radiant, glowing human figure moved and sang. It wasn't the same song or dance that she sang and danced when we first spotted her in the telescope or in our encounter with her on the orange-red plains of Mars. This time her voice was soft, flowing, and mellow. Instead of receiving joy from her, like we had before, we received heat. Soothing, comforting, thawing heat. Heat like on a summer day on Earth.

As the blue girl with blue-fire hair sang softly, a warm glowing substance appeared and covered Gabe's body like a warm blanket. Before we knew it, his body started rising up toward us. Instead of the zombie-like eyes and face, we saw Gabe's lively and sparkling face.

He held up his head in the darkness and said, "I'm coming up!"

His body followed his words as he shot upward like an elevator. Immediately after Gabe regained his composure, Austin also regained his whereabouts and came out of his coma-like state of hibernation. Next, Madison began to sing softly like the dancing and singing girl. Then, in the blink of an eye, the glimmering, bluish human figure vanished once again right before our eyes.

"I wonder if this girl is an angel or some kind of good spirit," I said.

"Well, if she is an angel, she's a high-tech angel," Gabe replied. "No wings for her...no dashes over the shoulder and big white robe. This is the 21st century, and she is in living color. Technicolor, in fact. With Blu-ray imaging."

She certainly wasn't Cupid, and she wasn't the archangel, Michael. She was the bluish-white, singing, and dancing girl . . . with supernatural powers to alter things and put miracles in motion with words.

When Austin came to himself and realized that we were still circling in midair, he hollered, "We're orbiting Neptune like the Moon or a satellite! Mervin Matthews' game has turned us into Neptune's 14th Moon."

It took me a minute, maybe two, to get Austin's point. It didn't matter to Austin because he wasn't letting the matter go.

Still hollering, he said, "Triton is one of Neptune's 13 moons and the largest of them. I think Mervin Matthews has tried to turn us into an orbiting moon. After all, it *is* his game."

"Neptune has thirteen moons, not fourteen," I said. "We can't become number fourteen! It doesn't even exist in the textbooks."

Then Austin hollered even louder, I mean very loudly. He was ticked-off loud.

"THAT'S IT! WE'RE OUT OF HERE! KNOWLEDGE JUST GOT US OUT!"

It's not hard to get Austin excited, especially when he makes a sudden discovery. He had just realized how the game worked. He finally got the hang of it. I mean, he really got the hang of it.

In less than a second, he hollered again, "Next episode!"

He was more than ready. He was back to being the go-to guy, "Mr. Strategy." Without delay, our bodies stopped spinning, speeding, and orbiting around Neptune like a satellite bird. Austin's words had power. Actually . . . each of us, our words had power.

CHAPTER 9

Racetracks and Saturn's Rings

Austin had called the last shot in Neptune and delivered us from that planet with his lightning-fast instincts, his science knowledge, and his words. But this time, it was going to take a whole lot more than instincts and knowledge. Our next adventure would require sheer courage in the face of evil

I can't say our next planetary episode was good or bad. However, I will say that the good *outweighed* the bad, and the chance to see and experience one of the most fantastic sights in the universe was worth it all! Now that's my opinion of the situation that I am about to share with you. Madison, Austin, and Gabe might not feel the same way. It turned out to be challenging, frightening, and, in street terms, we almost got our butts kicked. There is no need for me to hold back this gritty story. This is how it started.

After we vanished from Neptune, in a flash of a second, the four of us were standing on the spectacular rings of Saturn. I instinctively knew it was Saturn and announced it to the group.

"Really!?! Saturn!?!" Madison marveled. "Then, we need to count the rings around the planet because Saturn is not the only ringed planet in our solar system. Jupiter, Uranus, and Neptune also have rings—but their rings don't compare with Saturn's."

From my viewpoint, Saturn's rings looked like a massive race track. The rings are about 169,800 miles wide. That's really wide.

We found ourselves standing on one of the middle rings that surround Saturn, Ring C. There are seven rings altogether. When we looked down, we noticed that underneath our feet were ice particles. That's because Saturn's rings are made up of 99% ice particles, with a little dust and rock in between the particles. There are also wide gaps between each ring. That's what divides them. The gaps open right out into space. That's dangerous.

Then, out of nowhere, loud zooming sounds were coming our way. So, what followed next? Four huge, eye-candy purple Harley-Davidson motorcycles appeared. They rolled up right in front of our feet. At that moment, we found ourselves clothed with perfectly-fitted black leather jackets, gloves, and boots, along with shiny black helmets. We all stared at each other at the same time, realizing that we had also been equipped with the quick-thinking skill to ride motorcycles. It was clear . . . we were about to go somewhere, and something was about to happen.

Well, I've told you where we were, and you just heard what happened, but before I can go any further with this story, I am going to have to provide you with some more facts about Saturn and its rings. You see, you can't understand the story without knowing the facts.

You need to understand that Saturn's rings have a front side and a backside. One side faces the Sun. That side is also lit by the Sun. The other is the backlit side. The backlit side is darker and almost black. Remember that. Right now, we were on the light side of Ring C. The light side is safe. Good things happen in the light.

Saturn also has fifty-two known moons. The largest is Titan. Titan is the second-largest moon in our solar system. Titan's atmosphere is nitrogen-rich, similar to Earth's a long time ago. But Saturn is not like Earth or Titan. Here's the BIG DIFFERENCE . . . Saturn's magnetic field is 578 times more powerful than Earth's.

Saturn's rings are in the middle of Saturn's enormous magnetosphere. On Mars and Neptune, the solar system's winds influence things, but around Saturn, the magnetic fields influence things. Remember that.

I hope you are still following me because I am building a case. Remember, it would be hard for you to understand what I am about to tell you if you didn't understand the facts about this planet. Here is my last fact about Saturn. Have you ever heard of nocturnal animals? Nocturnal animals sleep during the day and are more active at night. You're probably familiar with some nocturnal animals like owls, bats, raccoons, and even rats. If not, you will be.

With Saturn's spectacular "racetrack" rings and the Harley-Davidson motorcycles right before us, we did what any normal teenager would do . . . we dragged raced in space. The motorcycles were finely-tuned and unusually loud on Ring C. Ring C was more than wide enough for us and billions more people. We were out in space terrain without any limits. No curfews. No speed limits. No boundaries.

We were all speeding. Gabe and Madison were in front. They kept going back and forth between being in first and second place. Madison's a girl, but she was managing to outrace us guys. We were fancy-free, teenaged space rangers racing around on the rings of Saturn. Free at last . . . but last didn't last long.

Gabe is adventurous, so he talked us into going on a journey to the dark side of Ring C. Dark means limited light and a few other things. We all had enough good judgment *not* to go to the dark side of the ring. We should have followed our judgment, instincts, and common sense. If our teachers or our parents were here, we wouldn't have even *thought* about taking such an unnecessary risk. But we had gotten caught up in being ... RANGERS!! *Space* rangers are not at all the same as *park* rangers.

We were riding on the dark side of Ring C. We felt brave and bold . . . above the stars. We were unstoppable. We were space rangers! Then we heard the zooming sounds of other motorcycles. We heard voices, too. We didn't want to believe it, but it sounded like a motorcycle gang was coming our way. As we turned around, we saw a bunch of human-sized rats. And, yes, they were riding motorcycles ... twice the size of ours. It wasn't fair. We didn't need a school bell to tell us it was time to start running, change classes, and go home.

As they got closer, we could see how tall the rats were. They looked like tall giants. They had tails like rats, flapping big ears, and big, snow cone-shaped noses like rats. But . . . Oh no! These rats were electrically-charged rodents. Saturn's magnetic field was energizing them. This was *not* good.

Exactly where in the universe did these space rats come from? They look ancient. They looked like a bad motorcycle gang that rose from the dead. This wasn't good. I believe they might have been from Titan.

Rats are pests. They don't have bones, so they probably wouldn't care if they broke our bones.

They were actually *chasing* us. And they looked ferocious *and* mad. Why were they chasing us like we were criminals? What did they want? And why did they look mad? Did they want to kill us? These space rats were on our tails. They were drag racing with us.

Madison was leading the pack. She usually likes to make friends and get to know people. She was speeding because she quickly realized that these rats didn't have it in them to be friends. You could see the stress written across her face as she struggled to stay ahead of the pack of rats. She was so stressed out that she'll probably never sing again.

Austin was right behind Madison. I thought that he would have come up with a strategy by now. Something. Anything. He couldn't come up with one for these space rats.

"Hey, Austin," I yelled. "Got any strategies for these space rats?"

"Not right this minute. I do know that we need an exterminator, and I'm not one!"

Gabe's mind wasn't working right, either. That's why he slowed down. Gabe was so scared of these giant rats that he wasn't even talking. I hoped he wouldn't go zombie on us again. Now was not the time.

These rats were trying to scare us to death. Dead isn't relevant when you're in space. You've already left Earth. So, where were they going with this? Look, I'm just trying to analyze this situation. This is a game. Why were they chasing us?

I wondered if this might be Mervin Matthews' alternative class, and the rats were his henchmen. Was he using them to try and scare the living daylights out of us? I could see how rats would want to cooperate with him. I bet you can see it, too. But wait a minute. They weren't trying to scare us. They actually wanted to harm us.

It seemed like there was no way off the "racetrack." As much as we wanted to, we couldn't leave the track. How would we get off, and where would we go, anyway? So, it seemed that Saturn has rings, a racetrack, and rats to make certain you keep moving, racing around forever.

Finally, with all the commotion going on, I just hollered, "Can a kid get a break around here?"

Right then and there, the rats stopped in their tracks, but only for a moment. They started chasing us again . . . with a vengeance. They were cruel. They started acting vicious. They were showcasing their teeth, and their enormous claws were showing as they started closing in on us.

Then they double-teamed us. They rode right up next to us, with a rat on each side of each one of us. They attempted to knock us off our bikes. One by one, they tried to grab us with their long, dirty claws, which were long enough to pull chunks of skin out of our bodies. They grabbed at our jackets. They grabbed mine. I needed to shut up. I had to remember that in this game, words have power. Whatever you say comes to pass.

Austin was knocked off his bike. I don't know how he managed to get back up and get away from them, but he did. On Earth, kids run and scream when they see rats and mice, but the rats end up running from them first. However, these rats weren't afraid of us, and they weren't about to run from us. What we were facing were space bullies. We should have stopped and fearlessly looked them in their eyes, ready to confront them, ready to fight our way out. Bullies tend to back down when someone confronts them and stands up to them.

Oh my God! Madison just fell off her bike. The rats knocked her off her bike. Now six huge rats were standing over her, surrounding her with their motorcycles. We had to go back. We didn't have a choice. We *had* to confront them. It was on. We weren't going to let them take out our friend, Madison. We came together, so we were leaving together. Before we reached her, one rat began to claw on her jacket. Fortunately for her, the leather was thick. They were so set on taking Madison down that they didn't see us approaching.

When the gruesome rats noticed we were right behind them, they seemed surprised that we had come back for Madison. Human beings care for each other. It was obvious that this thought and action was foreign to them. They came closer to us and eyeballed us one by one. They knew we were outnumbered. With their oversized, beady, black eyes, clothed in their dark gray, coarse hair, they began to give us an "it's-all-over-for-you" grin. The battle was becoming mind over matter.

This time it was me, instead of Austin, who took the lead. It didn't matter that the rats were seven feet tall, and ugly didn't count. I had heard that rats were intelligent, but I knew that they hadn't been to school because Mr. Matthews' brother wasn't allowed to teach anymore. They didn't show us any respect. Also, it was obvious that they didn't think the matter through because they stepped forward like they were about to jump us and beat us down.

The atmosphere was quiet. It was time for someone to make a move. We were standing face-to-face with an enemy. It was us or them. The rats couldn't figure out what we had up our sleeves, but they did sense that we weren't afraid anymore. The electrically-charged rodents also knew we were from another planet, but what they didn't know was… we understood the game. And we had some knowledge about them. And that made my mind jump into gear.

Like a madman, I hollered as loud as I could, "NOCTURNAL ANIMALS!"

It startled them. They froze. I seemed confident to them . . . not just confident, but bold. So, I fearlessly got right up in their faces and, with a crazy look on mine, looked them in their ugly eyes and hollered, like a madman, "LIGHT! LIGHTS! LET THERE BE LIGHTS!"

Soon as I said that, they took off. Boy, did they run!

The light broke forth like the morning. The light absorbed the darkness everywhere. As soon as the light hit them, they scattered like Earth rats.

My only response to their lack of courage was, "Really!"

After the rats disappeared, Gabe and I walked over to Madison to help her get up off the ground. She was somewhat shaken by the whole experience. Austin looked down at his leg, and he noticed that his pant leg was ripped from falling off the bike, and his leg was bleeding some.

He had a puzzled look on his face. He was puzzled by the sudden disappearance of the rats and questioned me about it.

"Why did the rats run when you yelled 'lights'?"

"Rats are nocturnal animals," I responded. "Nocturnal animals generally sleep during the day and are more active at night. They don't like the light."

There was nothing else left to say about the Rings of Saturn. We had mastered yet another game . . . through . . . instincts, scientific knowledge, and the power of our words.

We returned to the light side of Saturn's Ring C. The dark side of the ring had been like a brief ride through a haunted house. In spite of it all, the Rings of Saturn were still spectacular. Nevertheless, we were on to our next episode.

CHAPTER 10

Dream Flight

Austin collected himself and hollered, "Comfort . . . PLEASE. Luxury flying accommodations p-l-e-a-s-e."

In a flash, we found ourselves sitting comfortably in a spacious, private luxury jet, or spacecraft, to be exact. Austin's words had power, and so did mine. Austin, Gabe, and I were feeling like kings, and Madison was feeling like a queen. We leaned back into the soft-posh leather seats and let our minds and bodies relax. In the midst of all this luxury, our minds and bodies were still in a little bit of shock from our Saturn, Neptune, and Mars experiences.

My friends and I were now leaving Earth's solar system. As we glanced outside the spacecraft's window, we saw the Milky Way. Viewing the Milky Way's planets one by one from a distance was an overwhelming experience for us.

Madison summed up all our feelings when she said, "I can see Earth, but I can't see my state or home anymore. I am beginning to miss home. Just knowing we are traveling far from my family makes me miss home even more."

I guess I should turn my attention back to our space adventure. Adventures don't last forever, so when it's over, I'll be returning home.

There was no question about it. We were all ticked off with Mr. Matthews' brother, Mervin. And rightfully so. I said what the others were probably all thinking.

"If we were going to be propelled a million miles away from Earth and sent out into outer space . . . it should have been our choice. Being in the depths of the ocean and being a castaway on a remote tropical island was one thing, but this borders on criminal."

Emphatically, I continued.

"Our parents don't know where we are! How will they ever find us? I'm sure by now they are wondering where we are. I'm sure everybody's wondering where we are. What will our teachers say when we don't show up for school? It seems like *some*body didn't take that into consideration."

"The only good thing about our predicament right now is that we're together," Austin remarked.

"Yeah," I said, "but what's it going to sound like on the news when they say four kids disappeared while playing a video game? No one is going to believe that story."

"Our good reputations are going to be ruined. Everybody will see us as truants, runaways, or just a group of kids out of control. I can just forget about being on the student council or on the basketball or hockey teams. After this adventure, I doubt if my parents will even let me out of the house to walk the dog."

"If Mr. Matthews' brother wanted to send someone out in space, he should have stayed with NASA and gone himself. The kids in school referred to him as being a genius. His credentials and college grades were supposed to be outstanding . . . but so are those of mad scientists. Man."

"I agree," Madison sounded in. "The worst fool is a smart fool. My dad always said that degrees and education don't make a person. You still need to have character. Character is doing the right thing because it's right, even if no one is looking. And respecting other people's rights."

"Yeah. You just don't send students into outer space without their parent's consent or permission," Austin said.

"You're right," Madison replied. "You can't even go on a field trip without a permission slip. Oh, he probably didn't think we needed a permission slip for a video game."

Like Austin and Madison, I was frustrated by the situation, and I told them all about my short-term resolution to it all.

"When I get back home if I ever make it back," I said, "I am going to write a letter to my United States congressperson and ask them to have a congressional hearing on the regulations of the video game industry. I am going to request that Congress review the requirements for video game store ownership, too."

I could have gone on forever. I would have if Gabe hadn't interrupted me.

"Everything you just said sounds good and real preventive. But the truth of the matter is, that's not going to help us *now*."

"Well," I said. "Thank God our teacher taught us enough about science to give us the knowledge to make it through space exploration. We can't say the same for his brother."

We were in a safe place now. I really should have stopped complaining because things had shifted. Our space misfortune had become our good fortune in space. We were on the verge of experiencing breathtaking and life-changing events that would mark our young lives forever . . . we didn't even know it yet.

Our spacecraft was passing by thousands of stars and hundreds of new planets. It was surreal. The shapes and colors of the planets and stars were beyond the scope of our imagination. Without me even noticing it, my vengeful thoughts toward Mervin Matthews and what I would do to him when I returned to Earth vanished. This was no place for such negative thoughts. We had just begun the journey of our life.

This luxury spacecraft we were flying in represented a transition point for us. It was transporting us from all the dangerous games to the planet of our dreams, but we didn't know that yet, either.

105

The spacecraft resembled a military spacecraft or maybe a spacecraft for someone special . . . or for a real special occasion. From the outside, it was lustrous, a shining, silver-colored, larger-than-life, missile-shaped vehicle. We snuggled into our comfortable, soft leather seats, more than ready for a relaxing nap. As we were settling into our seats, a flight attendant walked over to us.

"Are you hungry?" he asked. "We're serving dinner now. Would you like buffalo wings, burritos, or pizza?"

We all answered at the same time.

"Yes! All three."

We were just that hungry. It didn't take long for us to finish eating our dinner. In fact, we gobbled it down. We had been suspended over Neptune without food or water for a long time.

Because time is measured differently in space-time from Earth time, we really weren't certain how long we had been on Mars, Neptune, and Saturn. Also, we had used up all our energy worrying about whether we were going to live or die in frosty, freezing weather or be swallowed up by poisonous vapors of gas.

Realizing that we had completed our meal, one of the three flight attendants headed back over to us and asked, "Dessert, anyone?"

The four of us said yes until she told us what was for dessert.

"We have ice cream today." In total agreement, we all hollered at the same time.

"No way!"

We had had enough of ice, cold temperatures, and any and all things cold. Austin, however, wasn't dismissing dessert altogether.

He looked at the attendant and said, "What about a hot fudge sundae?"

"One hot fudge sundae coming up."

We just looked at each other and laughed.

"Austin," I said. "You sure love to eat, even in space."

Talking about dessert made me think of my favorite homemade German chocolate cake and the way my mother makes it. So, I decided to ask for a slice of German chocolate cake. Since we were already in a fantasy world, I assumed the flight attendant would deliver me a near-perfect hunk of German Chocolate cake, and I was right. She did.

The décor of the luxury spacecraft helped us to quickly forget our near-death experiences. After Gabe and I had left the Abyss and the sunlight levels of the ocean, we laughed about it on the beach. However, Madison, Austin, Gabe, and I couldn't bring ourselves to laugh about what we had experienced around Neptune. Neptune was deathly cold and dark. If it hadn't been for the reappearance of the radiant, blue, singing, and dancing girl, we would have all been dead . . . and lost in space. Needless to say, we were more than ready to put all that behind us.

Although none of us had flown in a luxury aircraft before, Austin was acting like he was born to ride in them.

He even looked around and said, "You know. I plan on buying my own private jet someday."

I wouldn't doubt it. Austin was already thinking like a junior exec in school.

But this was no ordinary spacecraft. We were the only passengers on it, and we were being treated like royalty. The inside of the spacecraft looked like it was decorated for a Dubai prince. The seats were top-of-the-line leather. The drinking glasses were made of crystal, and the forks, knives, and spoons were gold. Every fifteen minutes or so, an attendant would come over to us and ask us if there was anything they could do to make us comfortable.

"May we help you in any way? What would you like now?" they constantly asked.

While we were enjoying our new-found, rich, and famous lifestyle, the co-pilot came out of the cockpit and welcomed us to the flight.

"Is there anything special I can do for you today?"

Madison didn't waste any time answering the pilot's question and questioning him.

"Yes. You can tell us where this spacecraft is going. What is our destination?"

The pilot replied, "I'm glad you asked that question. We travel by special request, so what's your request?"

Without asking any of us, Madison spoke right up.

"I heard that scientists have discovered over 500 new planets."

She paused for a second, then said the magic words.

"I would like to go to a highly advanced planet with life on it. A planet that's similar to Earth."

Gabe interrupted Madison's conversation by asking the pilot, "Is that possible?"

The co-pilot said, "There are hundreds of billions of galaxies in the universe. Surely, we can find a planet similar to Earth for you. It's our responsibility to make it possible. What's impossible with normal, everyday people is possible with us. You're on the right flight."

Madison, Austin, and Gabe just looked at each other hard and long. We all knew we were about to play the final game. Not only were we about to play the final game, but we were on a luxury spacecraft that obviously was a part of it.

The only difference this time around was . . . we knew how to control the game with our words, our knowledge, and our instincts. We were mastering the games. We were creating our own reality by our words. This was powerful to us. Could life be like this? Could words create circumstances or situations? A world? Even a universe? We were making a life-changing discovery . . . the creative power of words.

The pilots were actually flying us to our desired destination. Was this a dream? In our last three games, we were just injected into other realities, planets, and dimensions in an instant. We realized the course of the game had changed. So, we decided to relax and watch a movie on the luxury spacecraft's big-screen television and eat premium popcorn. We were living large.

It was time for us to take one last look at this galaxy before we soared away from it. From the spacecraft's windows, we saw the spectacular view of the Milky Way. As the spacecraft departed from the Milky Way's galaxy, we took one last glance at Earth. It looked smaller from our view and less significant. Maybe it *was* less significant at the point where we were in our lives.

We traveled through hundreds of other galaxies. The game was beginning to finally have its perks. The spacecraft flew from one galaxy to another, and as our eyes continued to stare out the windows, we studied the universe's stunning stars.

Before long, all of us, with the exception of Gabe, were fast asleep. We had a lot to dream about, and while we were dreaming in our seats, Gabe was living his dream. Gabe likes fast things. He wasn't about to pass up an opportunity to experience every moment of flying on a fast spacecraft. As soon as we closed our eyes, Gabe headed straight to the pilot's cockpit.

He took the opportunity to learn everything he could about flying from the experts. The pilot and the co-pilot took a special interest in Gabe, just like the Brazilian pilot that gave him his pilot's cap. While we were still asleep, they allowed Gabe to sit in the seat on the captain's right and fly with him. Gabe was a co-pilot for about ten minutes. He was thrilled and excited. He was hardly able to calm himself down when he finally did go back to his seat and join the rest of us in sleep. When we were all awake, he told us about the experience and that it was an experience that he would *never* forget.

In orbit, our dreams were a lot clearer and more colorful than on Earth. Our dreams were more frequent in space, too. For some reason or another, when you dream in space, you dream about things that are really important and dear to you. While I was dreaming, the bluish-white, airy, dancing girl appeared to me again. She was right outside the aircraft's window, just dancing slightly. She was following me in my dreams and in reality. This time, though, her appearance was slightly different. She was not only shimmering. She was *glimmering*.

Shimmering and glimmering aren't the same thing. Shimmering is like fourteen-karat gold, and glimmering is like twenty-four-karat gold. Twenty-four-karat gold is purer than fourteen karats. It has a higher gold content. It's a step up. There was a slight atmospheric change in the quality of her brightness when we left Earth's solar system. It caused her shimmering to be brighter and more intense. Her brightness was almost blinding. And very brilliant, like diamonds. It was so brilliant that I had to squint my eyes at the brightness. I almost could have used a pair of sunglasses.

When the spacecraft finally stopped, we were in an unknown place. Because we were still in a game, and this was a fantasy, we didn't need to walk through a door to exit the spacecraft. We were just there . . . wherever *there* was. We didn't awake from sleeping. We just appeared on a new planet from the place of our dreams. Our pilot looked at us and smiled. He said, "This is it. The Top."

CHAPTER 11

Einstein Minds

The four of us walked right into a winter wonderland. There was white, sparkling snow as far as we could see. There were also rays of light beaming from every direction and bouncing off of the snow. Everywhere we looked, there was pure, glistening white snow, and everything was covered with it.

We were so captivated by the beauty of the snow that we didn't notice that standing right in our path was a light grey male reindeer. He was massive, with huge antlers. He stood right in front of us, with his head held high and a friendly expression. The reindeer looked at us like he was expecting us. He must have been part of a welcoming committee.

By the looks of his clothes, he was definitely dressed for the part. He wore a red and white scarf that hung loosely around his neck. A bell was attached to the scarf. He stared directly at us, and then he winked. His wink was non-threatening and welcoming.

The snow continued to sparkle, portraying every facet of each snowflake like a diamond. Light bounced off of each facet and burst into a rainbow of brilliant colors as it hit each snowflake. The snow appeared fresh, but it wasn't really cold to touch. The rays of light continued to beam brightly from every direction.

There was a light blue, crystal-clear, frozen river in the middle of the vast winter landscape. It was glowing like glass on one side. Everything was glowing. The far-reaching, crystal-clear water reminded me of descriptions of the sweeping Nile River that runs through Egypt. In ancient Egypt, the Nile River was the source of life and transportation. Maybe this beautiful, crystal-clear, blue river was the source of life to this winter wonderland. We had no idea what lay ahead, but I sensed that with every step we took, it would grow more and more wondrous.

The reindeer never took his eyes away from us. He began to raise his massive head up and down, nodding as if he was giving us permission to do something. Then, in an Earth-like voice, to our surprise, the animal spoke.

"Go ahead. Stand on the river. Slide and skate on it."

I couldn't resist the urge. I was the first one to jump on the frozen river and slide. I started sliding down the river like a car driving down a highway. It was better than skateboarding.

When Madison and Austin realized it was safe, they joined in and followed me on the river. Gabe was the last one to join in on the adventure. He was hesitant because he wasn't familiar with frozen rivers. Or frozen anything, for that matter. Remember, Gabe was from a tropical climate. In his mind, ice resembled a glass mirror, and he had enough sense to realize that mirrors break.

Once he stepped onto the ice and realized that the river was frozen solid, his fear left. He found himself gliding and sliding with us, enjoying every moment of this completely new experience. However, for what we were about to experience, it didn't matter whether the river was frozen or not.

The river began to slope downward. Soon our bodies began to pick up speed. We zoomed past the landscape. We were going faster than we had planned to go. We were still having fun, but we seemed to be losing control. Our bodies were traveling pretty fast, maybe more than fifty miles an hour. It was a little scary, but we still felt safe. Although we were still moving, our bodies suddenly began to automatically slow down . . . on their own.

Before I could catch myself and stop, I found myself sliding toward the other side of the river. It had melted gradually, and I wasn't able to tell the difference between the ice and the water. There were two reasons for this. The first one was . . . I hadn't looked down at the water, and the second reason caught me totally by surprise.

When I realized what was going on, I hollered, "HEY! I'M WALKING ON WATER! REAL WATER! AND I'M NOT SINKING! I'M WALKING ON WATER!"

We were in the middle of the river, not on the side of it. A narrow current was moving swiftly through the middle of the river. The current was serving as a sailboat for our feet. The four of us were sliding on the swift-moving current as though it was ice. The current was carrying us.

We were in the middle of the river. I didn't think of turning around. I am glad I didn't. We continued to slide down the river, and before we knew it, the winter landscape had turned into spring.

Even though the world we arrived in looked like Earth, it wasn't like Earth. The laws of gravity weren't the same, at least not in this river. When we came to a stop, our feet gradually sank into knee-deep, warm water that swirled around us like a whirlwind.

This place, with its appearance of springtime, was awesome! Instead of snow, there were astounding, vivid colors everywhere. Every hue and tone surpassed anything I had ever seen on Earth. The landscape looked like it was color-matched to a large box of crayons. As we continued farther into springtime, the bright rays of light increased more and more.

The four of us stepped away from the moving current and came off to the side of the river to relax and play. The water was very inviting, captivating, and fascinating to us. In some respects, it reminded us of one of Earth's water parks. So, we just parked out on the side of the water.

This river was quite different from anything on Earth. It was life-changing and altering, although it took us a while to realize it. After we had played in the river and relaxed in it for a while, we got out. Our clothes were soaking wet, but it really didn't matter since it was warm outside. We laid out on the beautiful, velvety-soft carpet of green grass.

Suddenly, a strong wind came by like a huge hair dryer and blew our clothes completely dry. Yes. In an instant, we were completely dry. That's when we really realized . . . this place couldn't even be compared to Earth.

As if to bring clarity to what happened, Madison said, "That was a real blow dryer!"

We all laughed . . . except for Gabe. Instead of responding to what had just happened, Gabe chose to reflect inwardly for a moment. He was always thinking deeply about stuff.

Then he asked, "I wonder if our words have power here . . . they did on the other planets?"

"Well," Austin replied, "the wind responded to our wet clothes, and we had not asked it to. The wind actually responded to a need we had without us using any words."

"That means this place is on a higher level than Earth, Mars, Neptune, Saturn, and all the other planets of our solar system," Gabe reflected.

Although we didn't know it yet, the water had altered our bodies and minds. When we stepped out of the water, our bodies and minds had been re-created. Although nothing special had happened that we were able to observe with our eyes, at least not yet, we sensed an excitement as we looked around. The atmosphere was filled with joy. We were definitely in another dimension. We had no idea how far away we were from Earth or what time it was. There was no sense of time passing.

Unexpectedly and quite suddenly, on the bottom of our feet, we felt a warm, tingling sensation. The sensation moved from our feet up through our bodies and up to the top of our heads. Wow. I was able to put my right hand through my body without my body falling apart. To the best of my ability, in limited Earth vocabulary, I tried to describe what had happened after the warm sensation moved through our bodies.

"I believe that our earthly bodies have been altered. The composition of our earthly bodies has been altered to adapt to the life form of this planet."

"All I know," said Austin, "is that *something* has happened to us."

Astonished, Austin said, "Look, our bodies! We look like extra-terrestrial or celestial beings, like in the movies. Our bodies still have substance, but they're lighter. Our appearance is the same, but the weight has changed. Our bodies look like millions of moving particles fused perfectly together." After moving his feet up and down real fast, with a warm smile on his face, Austin said, "I can still feel the ground under my feet. And no . . . I can't see through Madison's clothes."

What Gabe asked next was only natural . . . at least for Gabe.

"I wonder if this means we can move faster, too."

His assumption was correct. Gabe's mind always took things to the next level very quickly.

The river was definitely a transformer. It contained the planet's life force. It was this planet's means of transformation for all newcomers. And that brings me to my next point. How many visitors have been here? Are we the first ones? Where is everyone else?

By now, we were a long distance from Winter Wonderland, and we were in the middle of Springland. The river sat in the middle of spring's landscape, the exact way it sat in the middle of Winter Wonderland. In Springland, it sat still like a crystal sea that reflects images like a mirror. The calm appearance of the water was very misleading because once the river captures your image... your life is never the same.

In the middle of our journey through Springland, I started to daydream about the radiant girl again. I pictured her standing right there in front of me. When the daydream ended, and my eyes got focused back on where we were, there, in her place, were four gigantic, silver-white, majestic horses. The enormous and stately horses were strapped in soft, black leather reins. By the very means of their arrival, we automatically knew they were there for us to ride.

The four of us climbed on the majestic horses without much difficulty. As soon as we were all saddled up and strapped in correctly, the horses dashed off onto the green plains. In mere seconds we had become expert horse riders . . . we had to . . . because it appeared that the horses were galloping over one hundred miles per minute. They were moving faster than we could wonder where we were going.

We were off on another journey. Through the lens of a camera, Madison, Austin, Gabe, and I looked like movie stars scripted to ride on a royal journey. But unlike movie stars, we didn't know the next scene. It really didn't matter that we didn't know where we were going. What we did know was that events had turned in our favor because each new episode introduced us to a new, dream-like world and experience. Now, we had come to realize that the bluish-white technicolor girl was leading and guiding us in the way we should go, and she was prospering our way.

Our horses flew through Springland. Soon we noticed that the thoughts in our minds had begun to fly, too. Our intelligence was increasing with the speed of the horses. I wondered what kind of horses these were. In a flash, I turned my head to the right. To my astonishment, I saw a large camp of celestial, glowing men riding on majestic, white horses, just like ours.

This camp of men appeared out of nowhere. Their faces and unmoving glances pointed forward as their horses rushed alongside us. Our horses and their horses were riding in sync with the same intensity and speed. The men didn't acknowledge us. They just kept moving alongside us. Then the riders and their horses vanished in a fiery whirlwind. Well, I guess there *are* men on this planet. The question is: what kind of men?

In the dash of their wind, we became teenage geniuses.

The river changed our bodies, but the horses changed our mental capacities. Something just happened that we couldn't explain. This was not an Earthly occurrence by any means.

Mathematical equations started appearing in midair before my eyes . . . mathematical equations on a college level. My mind started solving the equations and figuring out answers to world hunger. But the transformation wasn't happening only to me.

Madison started shouting with excitement.

"My mind has started formulating cures for cancer!"

Gabe was beyond excited.

"And I've figured out why the spacecraft that flew us here worked like a rocket while it was in space! This is unbelievable!"

Austin had come up with ways to improve Earth's environment and had singled out some strategies for world peace. We had been transformed into superhuman beings. We were speeding through

Springland at the speed of light, and our minds were thinking, analyzing, and calculating at the speed of light, too. We had become teenage Einsteins!

When the horses came to a halt, we were more than ready to rest. They stopped in the middle of a deep green forest. The forest was next to the same crystal-clear, blue water that had carried us from the sparkling, snow-covered Winter Wonderland to the brightness of Springland. We climbed off our horses and sat down on the beautiful, soft grass for a while. The grass felt like velvet as we brushed our fingers over it. It was so comfortable, still, and peaceful that we almost dozed off to sleep.

Our bodies weren't tired from the ride. It was our minds. Our minds were exhausted from our elevated thinking and the rapid change which had occurred in our brains. It was almost as if our brain cells had been rearranged, and we were processing information at an astounding rate, even faster than a computer.

We were able to take in a few deep breaths of fresh air. The air strengthened us. Like everything else on this planet, the air even possessed a unique quality. The air strengthened us like food. Go figure!

Every planet and every place has unique characteristics that distinguish it. It seemed that, here on this planet, the unique characteristics were joy and light. I had never experienced this kind of joy on Earth. This joy made me feel alive and strong, more alive than I had ever felt. If I could box it up and take it back to Earth, I would. This joy didn't come from the people you had met, and it didn't come from the things I did or experienced here. It was in the atmosphere. The atmosphere was full of the solid presence of joy. It was part of the air.

As we rode forward from Springland, we entered into the Land of Summer. Our eyes could see that the atmosphere and everything around us was becoming more brilliant. This brilliance, like the joy we had experienced in Springland, was beyond our earthly comprehension or description. The luster and intensity continued to increase as we rode on. Although the light became brighter, it didn't produce more heat. We were comfortably warm.

The illuminating light was everywhere. Noticeably, oddly, and surprisingly, there was no sun in the sky. Our science class hadn't provided us with answers to *this* phenomenon. How could there be warmth without the sun's rays? The warm, radiant light was continuing to surround us. The light was wonderful. It made this world feel perfect, like Utopia. It *was* perfect.

The trees, plants, and flowers were fascinating. They were real, but they didn't seem real. The plants and tree leaves were a rich and deep green color. There is no way I can describe this right other than the trees, plants, and flowers were alive. They had the form of trees and plants, but the very, very small particles they were made of were moving while staying in place. I would not have been surprised if they started talking, although they didn't.

After we had fully scoped out our new surroundings, we noticed that there was something unusual about all of our faces. There was very fine, powdery, gold dust on our skin tones of cream, tan, golden brown, and brown faces. The very fine, gold dust had covered our clothes and hands, as well. What was the meaning of this?

Perhaps the gold dust was symbolic of the place where we had arrived. Perhaps the gold dust was a reflection of the illumination in our minds. Maybe it was connected to the intense shafts of light in the atmosphere. One thing for certain, this place was full of light, and there was no darkness in it at all. The closest I can come to describing this new-found Land of Summer is that it was ten times the beauty that I had imagined in books I had read about the Hawaiian Islands, with their volcanic dust. But this place did not have volcanic dust. It had *gold* dust.

CHAPTER 12
Serapha

For a moment, I just felt like singing. No real reason. I just felt like it. This was the kind of place where I expected the radiant, bluish-white girl to arrive on the scene . . . singing. But instead of her, we heard birds singing. In fact, the singing was coming from some beautiful bluebirds.

The singing birds must have sparked something in Madison's new, re-created brain because before we knew it, she started singing, too. She wasn't just singing. She was making up songs and sounds as she sang. It was beautiful, and she was in perfect harmony and sync with the bluebirds.

Her lyrics were good enough to win a Grammy. I didn't know Madison had it like that. Neither did Austin. It's strange how you can be friends with someone for a long time and still not know everything about them.

What happened next was only natural, at least for our new surroundings and everything else that had taken place. Like the birds caused Madison to sing, Madison's voice must have called the glimmering girl to reappear. The radiant girl showed up. She appeared to be dancing and singing to Madison's song. She knew the song. Don't ask me how. The radiant girl didn't say hello. She didn't talk. She just started singing and dancing. When Madison stopped singing and dancing, the girl stopped singing and dancing. She just smiled and looked at us as if she was waiting for us to say we were pleased with the planet's breathtaking summer surroundings.

Maybe this was her home. That would explain why she glowed all the time. Maybe she was our orbit tour guide, who had finally caught up with us again. Perhaps she was appointed to us on Earth and followed us to this planet for a special reason. She would appear and disappear like the riders on the white horses. It's conceivable that she is invisible and never really leaves us or forsakes us. She seems to make herself visible to us at her own will.

Our bodies and minds were extra-terrestrial, but we still didn't have the DNA of this planet or her. That's PROBABLY why we couldn't figure SOME THINGS OUT ABOUT her OR THE PLANET. One thing we knew for certain was… this was definitely a planet of light.

In her presence, we began to think about the things we desired and enjoyed the most. Within moments, each one of us found ourselves with a baseball and a glove in our hands. The bluish-white, glimmering girl also had a baseball and glove in her hand. She threw the ball at a distance, and the ball circled back to her like a boomerang.

She was playing a perfect game of catch all alone. Then out of nowhere, a baseball landed in my hand. I clutched the ball and played, too. I threw the ball. It came back to me on its own, and I caught it. I looked at our guest and smiled. She smiled right back at me, although she didn't invite me into her game.

Next, Austin raised his hands in the air as if to motion the universe and said, "Bring it on." Right then and there, three baseballs landed smoothly right into the magical gloves that appeared on Austin, Madison, and Gabe's hands.

Austin remarked, "I can get used to this. It's always a perfect pitch and catch. Pure speed. It's like we're in seventh heaven."

"The magical baseballs move even faster than the majestic horses," Gabe said.

From the way, she smiled at us and indirectly invited us to play the same game *and* provided the gear, we decided that this time the radiant girl was willing and ready to communicate with us. Our minds had been renewed and conformed to the intelligence of the planet. We were thinking and communicating on a higher level . . . her level. And the level of what appeared to be her planet. The blue girl finally spoke.

"I've been with you all the time, and I have been following you from the moment you ventured out into orbit. Your travels and trials have not been in vain and without purpose. This is the Top of the

Universe. Your thoughts have brought you here for a universal purpose. Come follow me . . . there are things you must see and learn about the future."

I was curious but comfortable with the glimmering girl. I had some questions for her and about her. Like . . . where's your folks? Your family? Your friends? Could she be all alone up here? She gestured MOTIONS for us to follow her, and before we knew it, we were again following our "orbit tour guide," this time through the Land of Summer.

As we walked, Austin whispered, "She really hasn't told us where we're going. We should have asked."

"I just assumed that we were safe. After all, she has come to our rescue twice and invited us into her game. Plus, she said she's been with us all along our journey," I replied quietly.

Nothing in our immediate environment signaled we were in danger. Madison, Austin, and I were counting on the orbit tour guides leading to continue on to the Top of the Universe.

There's nothing like looking into your friend's face to get reassurance when you're walking into unfamiliar territory. As we continued walking, Austin kept looking around at Madison and me. I could tell he was trying to make eye contact with us to see if we were all thinking the same thing.

Finally, he whispered, "Are we safe? Are we?"

For a while, we were just trying to be respectful and polite. But the truth of the matter was . . . we all had a whole lot of questions. And who said we couldn't ask questions or talk on a tour? We might as well start talking now.

We didn't know how long it would take us to get to our next destination. What's more, we didn't know how long the bluish-white girl would be with us. She might vanish at any moment like she seemed to be in the habit of doing.

"Austin is right," Gabe said. "We're following her like she's a high school principal, and we have to go to the office."

Austin and Gabe were both spot-on. She wasn't a school principal or a teacher. She wasn't even an adult. So why were we acting scared and not talking? She was a girl, a teenager like us . . . well . . . kind of, but not quite. Madison looked around at me as we were walking. I could tell she was thinking the same thing I was thinking. Besides, Madison can only be quiet for so long. So, she broke the ice and asked the bluish-white girl the first question.

"Is it ok if we ask you your name?"

"Sure. I am Serapha," answered the glimmering girl.

Next, Madison asked, "Would you like to know our names?"

"I already know your names. Madison, Austin, Gabe, and Anton. Right?" In agreement, we all nodded and said, "Yep."

We were a little taken off guard that she knew our names. I guess it showed on our faces. Serapha relaxed and smiled a warm smile.

That relaxed us, too. She opened up. "This is the Top of the Universe. We know all things, and we can show you things to come."

Austin was listening attentively. He always crunched up his brow whenever he was listening attentively. He still couldn't understand why his re-created brain kept blocking simple information about the planet. So, his next question to Serapha was only natural.

"We? Who are *we*?

"The Universal Residents," she replied.

Serapha's answer really got Austin started.

"Universal Residents!?! Exactly who are they? Are the Top of the Universe's residents here adults? Teenagers? Other kinds of beings? Who *are* the Universal Residents?"

Calmly, Serapha answered, "There's no age or time at the Top of the Universe. We're not like Earth. We conduct our lives with wisdom and knowledge. There are different levels of wisdom and learning. We're forever learning. We learn here like you grow on Earth. Everyone has the same opportunity and capacity. I think on Earth, you call it the 'ability to learn'. We're at a higher level than human beings on Earth. We have within us a spirit of wisdom and revelation. It's like a river flowing on the inside of us. It's a river of seeing and knowing things. Things present as well as things to come. There's a constant flow."

Serapha's thoughts were obviously on a higher and much more advanced level than our thoughts. Her ways and the ways of her planet were superior to Earth's ways. That's why Austin couldn't respond to her answers, and Madison didn't ask any more questions.

Unlike Austin and Madison, Gabe remained silent. He was using our walk as a time to reflect and observe as we made our way to the Top of the Universe. The real truth is… Gabe's mind was overloaded. The events of our entire solar journey had packed his mind like the suitcase he packed to come to America. Now, he wasn't in a zombie-like state as he was on Neptune and the Abyss of the ocean. I could tell, though, that he was just turning things over and over in his mind. After a period of silence, Gabe spoke.

"Just in case you're wondering why I haven't said anything. There's never a need to ask questions about a movie when the movie is still going on. I figured everything would reveal itself as we moved forward on our journey."

Gabe was right because, to our left and right, there stood lush, wonderful scenes and scenery like we had never witnessed on Earth. There were glowing, enormous, magnificent banana and mango trees and oversized tropical plants that radiated light.

With a look of delight on his face, Gabe nodded his head gently and said, "We are in a sweet spot."

When I looked at the rich, colorful plants and trees, my Einstein mind kept ticking . . . *scientific medical discoveries*. I knew something was there. That's why I could not help but wonder what type of plants we were seeing. I could sense life and healing in them. If breathing the Top of the Universe's air was like food to our bodies, and its water had transformed our brains and bodies, there was no telling how these plants might benefit and improve life on Earth.

I perceived that major medical discoveries were right here before our very eyes. I saw Earthly solutions but not the Top of the Universe's solutions. Why did there seem to be a veil over our minds when it came to interacting with the dynamics of this planet?

On the Top of the Universe, we saw only partially, and we knew things only partially. We rarely seemed to get the whole picture. Maybe there was a hidden plan for us not to get overly attached to this planet and not want to go back home to Earth. Just thinking.

Austin wanted to know more about the Universal Residents. I wanted to understand what kind of plants we were looking at and what they were capable of healing. Perhaps they might be used for medicine? What were they using for medicine? Was anyone on this planet ever sick, or was sickness and disease non-existent here?

On Earth, most medicines are made from plants. I could only imagine what these plants and the other stuff on this planet could cure. If these plants could be used to cure sickness and diseases, maybe Serapha would allow me to take a few plant seeds back to Earth. That's not a far-out thought. Americans, international scientists, and astronauts have been in space for years studying life and physical sciences.

There's an international space station right above Earth today. This space station has astronauts and scientists living on it. They are from a number of different countries. The United States has crew members there, too.

One day when I was in the library, I read a scientific magazine that said that doctors had conducted laboratory experiments on the international space station. One experiment was trying to find cures for diseases of the human body. Another experiment explored a new way to increase Earth's fuel supply with alternative energy sources.

Scientists give the impression that microgravity might accelerate the effects of their research findings. If you had asked me what "microgravity" meant before I rode on the massive, majestic, silver-white horses or swam in the life-changing, crystal-blue water, I would have told you to go talk with my science teacher, Mr. Matthews. You still might need to talk to Mr. Matthews, but at least I can now have an intelligent conversation about it.

Now I somewhat understand the concept. Certain extreme environments alter the cell expression in humans, animals, and plants. I don't know how science teachers on Earth are teaching such a complicated topic, but maybe they're leaving those subjects to the space scientists. The long and short of is . . . cell expression in humans, animals, and plants act differently in space . . . things speed up there.

Wait a minute! Mervin Matthews worked at NASA. We're supposed to be playing a video game, but this is not a game. We've passed the game stage. We have surpassed the international space station by going outside of our solar system and the world as we know it. And the question now in all of our heads was . . . what might be the connection between Mervin Matthews and this place?

"I bet if our science teacher was here, he would have been more than just a space tourist. He would have made this Top of the Universe experience a learning adventure," I said out loud.

I turned to Austin and whispered, "I'm going to try and take some of these plant seeds. They can probably be used for some scientific research project on Earth. My pants pocket is a safe place to store them. One of these plants is bound to have some life-saving compounds inside them. They might be a miracle drug for Earth."

"How do you even know if these plants will grow on Earth?" Austin asked.

"We won't know unless we try it."

I paused from walking and reached over into the patch of plants and tried to break off a plant stem. It should have been easy because the stem was slim and soft. But no matter how hard I tried, the stem wouldn't break. It resisted my efforts. When I stopped trying to break it off . . . the whole plant bounced right back into place like it was alive. It was right there and then . . . that I knew I was on to something with these plants. If I couldn't get a plant stem, I was going to try a simpler task like getting seeds out of the flower; that should have been easier. I tried pulling out a couple of seeds from a flower. It was like pulling teeth. The seeds didn't want to come out.

I hadn't realized it, but when I stopped walking, Austin had stopped, too. He stood back and watched me struggle to break a simple stem and gather a couple of seeds. My failure with such a small task made him laugh uncontrollably.

After Austin finished laughing at my efforts, he said, "When all else fails, remember the rules of the game. This game is based on knowledge, instincts, and words. Your words have power. Your words move things."

After saying this, Austin left me and ran and caught up with the rest of the group.

Our group was still following Serapha through the Land of Summer. Bright shafts of light were still shining amazingly throughout the entire landscape. This was definitely a different world. There was no chance of me getting lost here . . . but I still ran quickly to catch up with the group.

In many respects, Serapha reminded me of our science teacher, Mr. Matthews, who was our trusted teacher and life guide. Inwardly, we felt like he always did those things that were in our best interest, like giving us a science project during spring break so that we could stay in a learning mode. She, like Mr. Matthews, seemed to gently push us to stretch our minds, increase our ability to comprehend, and expand our horizons.

Like Mr. Matthews, Serapha said, "You should never stop learning. Although it doesn't seem to make sense to learn and study so much today, it will make sense and be valuable to you in the future."

Serapha definitely was speaking Mr. Matthews' language. She said there were things we must see and learn for the future. I wondered if this girl was about to try to enroll us in the Top of the Universe school. Imagine attending school on an advanced planet. That would take learning to a whole new level. Maybe I would come back to Earth on top or just get some meaning to my life. Serapha was starting to get real serious. She reminded us that we had come to the Top of the Universe for a purpose. Unless I missed it, she really hadn't established this before. Well, it didn't take a noble purpose to get us here. I didn't need a noble purpose to play a video game or take the vacation of a lifetime. I was, however, willing to listen to her story. The idea of having a purpose was captivating. At least she's included us in Earth's plans for the future.

I haven't forgotten about the plant seeds. In fact, I had decided to talk to the plants and ask them if they could heal human bodies, and, if so, what did they heal? That wasn't so strange; I thought… at least not for this planet.

A very famous American scientist and inventor in the early 1900s, George Washington Carver, used to talk to plants and flowers. He lived many years ago, and he made great contributions to American agriculture and science. He discovered hundreds of inventions from plants and vegetables that are now used all around the world. No one laughed at his discoveries and inventions. In fact, he was invited to speak all over the world. He said the secret to discovering the many secrets locked inside plants was to love them and communicate with them.

If students on planet Earth could dissect a plant and a frog in a science class, surely my new, re-created, lighting-fast mind should be able to analyze the purpose of a plant on the Top of the Universe. Would they let me? Would the plants unlock their secrets to me, like they did to Dr. Carver?

I decided to take a step forward and try communication with the plants. The thought came to me that if I concentrated on the plants long enough, they might open up their secrets to me. It was a matter of mind over matter, and in this world and place, that seemed to work.

On Earth, it's called observation and extrasensory communication. However, on this planet, it's called being on top of your game - being in sync with the universe and extracting or pulling information out of a person, plant, or situation for a higher purpose. In my teacher's world, this would simply be called science.

CHAPTER 13

Castles in the Sky

We were still stunned by our newly-created bodies, our heightened intelligence, and our far-reaching imaginations, but this was small compared to what we would see and learn in the Land of Summer.

I've heard of castles in the sky, but I have never heard of elevators and escalators in the sky. At this point, what I had heard and what I had seen didn't matter. As we were walking, right before our very eyes appeared a gold-plated elevator and a gold-plated escalator in the sky.

It was obvious the gold-plated elevator and the gold-plated escalator had a purpose. On Earth, escalators take you to the second, third, and fourth floors of a super mall. And elevators take you up in three-story and high-rise buildings.

The gold-plated elevators and the gold-plated escalators were going up and down. The doors of the elevator were opening and closing. However, there was no one getting on or off of them. We could hear voices, though. The voices were speaking English. Well, were they really speaking English, or were our re-created minds interpreting their language at lightning speed into English?

As we continued to walk with Serapha, our eyes were unquestionably fixed upon towns and cities in the air. We were spellbound by them. The cities, or whatever they were called, were multi-leveled. They were stacked one on top of the other, level upon level. They lit up the sky.

On Earth, the streets and roads are all on the ground's surface. However, here there was no single ground surface. There were as many ground surfaces as there were levels. Go figure that.

In the distance, I could see houses and buildings. They looked like the kind of houses and buildings you would only see in a dream.

There were perfectly lined streets with perfectly shaped trees. There were bushes and flowers everywhere. The trees and flowers swayed back and forth gently like they wanted to dance. Their colors were rich and full, almost juicy looking, like candy. Very inviting. What a world!

It's quite likely that there were people living in the buildings and homes. If there were people living here, what would they look like? What would they be like? What kind of people, or beings, lived on this planet? *That* was the real question.

By now, Gabe had enough information, so he decided to ask Serapha the question that we were all thinking.

"Are there people in these cities?"

"Yes, there are people all over the cities and all over the seasons," she replied.

"Why could we hear them but not see them?" Gabe asked.

"Your minds have been re-created and renewed, but your bodies are not fully transformed. If we converted your bodies into the complete nature of the Top of the Universe, you would have to stay here forever. And since you have to return to Earth at some point, it is not possible to carry out a full transformation.

"You may be able to see *some* substances and elements such as plants, animals, and solid buildings, but some of your senses are limited here. You do not have fully activated senses to see in the realm of the higher life."

Austin was overly excited by the cities and high-rise buildings in the sky.

"This is so cool," he said. "One level looks like a clean New York City. The other level looks like a suburb with luxury cribs. Look over there! That has to be a Miami look-a-like!"

Serapha was a little confused by his language.

She said, "Excuse me . . . explain."

Austin quickly understood that slang talk was not a part of her vocabulary.

He replied, "I meant mansions and houses."

"Ok. Now I understand," she said, smiling. Then she went on to explain some things in her world.

"You can't see the Universal Residents, but they can see you. If you had more light working inside you, you would be able to see them with your naked eye. They can hear, see, observe, and touch you, though. If you had greater light working on the inside of you, you would be able to see them, too."

"I don't get it," Gabe said. "Our minds and bodies were re-created to fit the planet. Why can't we see its people?"

"You still have remnants of Earth's darkness," Serapha answered. "Your memories and images of things like wars, suffering, crimes, natural disasters, hate, fear, and pain prevent you from seeing fully. Although you have some Light in your world, you still don't have enough to see everything here. This is a planet of Light. There's no darkness here. We walk in total light."

"Will we ever be able to see them?" Gabe asked.

"Perhaps you will one day, but for now, you are used to seeing darkness on Earth. The darkness blinds you. However, it will pass away one day. Some light is already shining there."

"I don't get it. What does darkness and light have to do with us seeing the people of this planet?" Gabe asked.

"Darkness blinds the eyes. It prevents you from seeing. It's not you. You yourself are not dark… you came from a planet that has a lot of darkness; it spots you. You see in part and know in part."

I asked the next logical question.

"Well, why can we see you and not them?"

"Because I'm on assignment."

In an instant, we found ourselves doing more than just observing the escalators and elevators going up and down between the levels. We found ourselves on an escalator, going up into the air. As we moved up through the sky, illuminating shafts of light continued to radiate everywhere.

I felt like I was in a big shopping mall with levels. Like stores in a shopping mall, each city level had a distinct personality of its own. There were mansions and houses on each level. Similar to Earth, there were street signs on every corner in every city. But there were no street lights or cars.

This place had to be the Top of the Universe because there didn't seem to be a top in sight. The height and width of the place seemed to go on and on forever. It was so vast that its sheer size was difficult to comprehend or grasp.

There was about a mile between each level. One level looked like the suburbs with spacious yards. Another level appeared to be designed for urban city dwellers and people who liked high-rises. We passed by one level that had roaming countrysides with farmhouses and barns. There was no shortage of space on this planet.

Serapha escorted us off the escalator to Level Seven. On Level Seven, there were spectacular bedroom homes. She escorted us to one home with a bubbly fountain in the front yard. When we arrived at the door, it was opened, and a deep voice came from inside.

"Hello".

To our natural eyes, this person was invisible. We couldn't see this person, but we could hear movement and feel the person's warmth. How did we know we could feel the person? Because the person who opened the door, a man to be exact, reached out his hand to us and shook our hands. His hand felt like an Earth hand. It was warm and had flesh on it. It had fine, thin, smooth fingers that felt warm. The fingers had a tingling sensation.

As the man made contact with our hands, there were sparks and flashes of white, radiant light that radiated from the point of contact. It wasn't blue like the bluish-white, glimmering light that we had observed on Serapha. It was a different kind of light. A more intense light. The touch was like a little spark on our skin.

A lot of things were unusual about this whole encounter. First of all, our elevated minds allowed us to see how people actually looked without seeing them. We had the ability to see what existed without seeing it. Go figure. Their images were inside our minds. This was what you called having eyes inside your head or a REAL LIVE IMAGINATION. The possibility of this type of thinking was enormous and far-reaching. Perhaps we could literally pull in what we saw and print the image of it on our minds. Maybe this was how young kids imagined that they would become famous entertainers one day.

I was beginning to believe that you could have what you imagined. You see it in your mind's eye. You embrace the thought or image. It incubates, becomes more and more real the longer you "see" it, and then, like a hen that sits on her eggs and hatches them, your thoughts or images "hatch." The thoughts or images materialize. You carry them out, or they direct what you do. Perhaps we could really pull in what we see, like a person pulling in a fish with a fishing pole.

It's good there's no darkness here. Things could get really dangerous and ugly if bad people were allowed to get away with their imaginations. Anyway, there's no need for me to go off the deep end in thinking. We're on the Top of the Universe. There's *only* light here.

At this point, we continued to be escorted through the Land of Summer by Serapha. She definitely fit into this place. Although one of the Universal Residents met us at the front door of one of the houses, we still felt like home invaders. We began to walk through our first large mansion in the sky with what appeared to be an invisible man.

This mansion was literally out-of-this-world, at least for four teenagers like us. As we walked through the mansion, we were escorted to an Olympic-sized swimming pool on one side of the enclosed backyard. On the other side was the season of winter. No joke… there was a ski slope with snowboards and skis at the bottom of the slope. This mansion had two seasons, summer and winter. We're really talking about a different world here.

We finished what we thought was the end of our home tour. Then . . . we were brought to the entrance of a spacious video game room the size of my entire home. The video game room was called "Games of the Future Room."

Before Madison could catch herself, she hollered, "Wait a minute! Didn't the video game store have a room with the same name? Go figure that."

Before we could take one step forward, the man who appeared invisible to us said in a deep voice. "I bet you like this."

He was right. The game room was full of the latest video game systems. The games were from Earth, the Top of the Universe, and there were other games I didn't know anything about. I guess Mervin Matthews didn't know about some of these games either because they weren't at his game store.

I had never seen or witnessed any of the Top of Universe's video games before. There were no games like them any place on Earth, or, at least, not in the game stores I went to. They were mind-boggling. Very fast. Not as fast as the majestic, silver-white horses... but close.

I was also beginning to wonder if Earth's video systems and games originated here. I was just thinking. However, if I see a street called Xbox Avenue, I'll let you know.

Madison, Austin, Gabe, and I didn't ask or receive permission to play the video games; we just "knew" it was ok to play. We figured if

Serapha knew our names without asking, the owner of this house for sure, knew we were gamers. Not just any gamers, but some of the best gamers in our entire school.

We picked up the lightweight controllers and played a Top of the Universe video game. We didn't abuse our privilege or take advantage of the hospitality. We played for quite a while, but it only felt like a moment. And the space speed of the games made us hungry.

I bet you want to know the name of the video game that we played on the Top of the Universe, don't you? It was called "Sky Rider." By the way, Madison and Austin won the game.

Before we could start round two, Serapha signaled to us that it was time to go. It was time to continue our journey to a place called the Archives. This was a first. I had never heard her mention the Archives.

Nodding her head up and down, she said, "The Archives is a good place. It has a purpose, and it's your final destination on the Top of the Universe."

Going down the elevator was different from riding up the escalator. We walked out the door and headed toward the gold-plated escalator. Before we could step on it, Serapha was redirecting us to the gold-plated elevator. It really didn't matter to us which one we rode down. They both had spectacular, scenic views, with a sense of weightlessness that reminded us that we were in space.

Up until this point, Serapha had been our helper on Mars, our strengthener on Neptune, and our standby and guide in the Land of Summer. Now she was about to show us some things to come.

There were so many different aspects of her personality. And still, we really didn't know where she had come from and who she was. We weren't certain that she was connected to this planet that she called the Top of the Universe.

So far, Serapha had led us on the right path. There was no reason to stop following her now. As we were heading to our final destination, all of a sudden, we began to move swiftly as we walked through the Land of Summer. We dashed non-stop through scenic bird reservoirs, lush tropical forests, and mountainous areas near streaming lakes. It was like being on a speed bike. It was obvious our tour guide knew where she was heading and had been there before. Why was she rushing? Why the change in her pace?

"I believe things are about to get eventful . . . again!" I shouted.

CHAPTER 14

Archives

Our purpose for going to the Top of the Universe was about to be revealed. Madison, Austin, Gabe, and I were on the verge of experiencing an encounter that would change the course of our lives and the course of our nation. This was serious.

As we continued to walk rapidly behind Serapha, we realized that she was escorting us to our destination with destiny. A gold-plated gate stood at the entry point of a complex. Directly inside the gate was a sea of magnificent palm trees. The palm trees appeared to go on forever. They were situated on deep, green, lush grass that looked like it had never been touched.

As we approached the end of the clusters of palm trees, we saw a huge halo of light. Behind the light was an enormous, shiny building standing before us. The shiny building looked like glass. However, the material it was made from wasn't any Earthly material that we were familiar with.

The building had a modern, high-tech look to it. On one hand, it looked like a big city library; on the other hand, it looked like an art museum. It definitely didn't look like a school building. Anyway, from the outside, the building looked like some scientific experiment might be going on inside. Currents radiated from the building. It made me wonder . . . what's going to happen to us when we get in there.

We looked at Serapha to get some hint of what might be going on or what we could expect to happen *after we entered the building*. She was shining. As for us, there was gold dust on our faces and hands. I was thinking that we didn't need any more changes. I had to get back to Earth. I didn't need to get back to school looking unrecognizable or like a gold, stardust boy. I happened to like the way I looked.

The shining building that stood before us looked like a spaceship. On Earth, the sun shines down from the sky on buildings, but here the light was coming from the building itself. It looked like a massive halo was hanging over it. We were captivated, mesmerized, and gripped by the very image of this building. We didn't know whether to run or stand still. Yet, it felt like the building was prompting us to come.

Serapha kept walking like there was nothing the matter. When she realized that we had stopped following her, she turned around and raised her arms, and said, "What's the matter?" I just looked at her and said, "You know what the matter is. Please explain to us why that building is glowing. What's making it glow? Give us a guarantee that we won't be glowing when we walk out of it."

I got nervous all over again. This could have been a setup or a trap. And we could fall for it because a friendly teenage girl who could sing and dance was used to bait us. I looked at Austin to see if he had a plan. He just stood still in silence. Gabe and Madison were like me. They just stood there waiting for Serapha, who was supposed to be our friend, to answer my questions. By now, Serapha should have answered my questions, but she didn't. She kept quiet. In her silence, she was studying the situation.

Then she took a hard look at us and said, "You're afraid . . . of the building. That's it. Don't be afraid. This is the Archives building. The Archives hold the past, present, and future information of the entire universe. The past and present are important, but the future is prized and precious. It's in motion. I have a question for you. Have you ever thought of impacting the future of your country and the world?"

To myself, I thought *I hadn't even made it out of high school yet.*

Shaking his head and waving his hand back and forth, Austin stepped back and said, "This has gone too far! How do we really know she's a teenager? She could be a transforming space creature."

Madison was speaking with all her heart, and she sincerely replied, "Wait. Listen. Believe me. She's okay. Trust me."

The sincerity in Madison's voice and her gentle plea to trust our new-found friend really touched Austin… so much so that he decided to give Serapha another chance to explain herself. Even Gabe and I were ready to listen carefully to her story without the presence of fear.

Serapha hadn't heard everything that Austin had said, but she could see and feel his concern and hesitation. She sensed our hesitation, as well. Trying to comfort us, she spoke in a very calm voice.

"The light surrounding the building is coming from the information stored inside the building. It's a treasure. It's the past, present, and future knowledge of human beings. There is no need to be afraid. There are no fear, danger, or enemies here. Things are peaceful here.

"Every once in a while, we are able to sway visitors that come here to try to change the course of events for the future of mankind on different planets. Sometimes we are successful. Sometimes we aren't. People have free will. There were times when we could influence people and change the course of events and the future. When there *is* that possibility, however, we make an attempt. That's why you're here today."

After her reassuring speech, Serapha smiled softly and said, "Follow me."

We believed her. So, we followed her.

From the moment she entered the modern building, she started to carry herself like a real adult. At that point, everything she said and did was official and proper. We all got the feeling that she was representing someone other than herself. Maybe she was being watched now that she was in the building.

When we were outside the building, we couldn't see into the building. However, once we were inside, we could see outside the building. We were also able to see through all the rooms in the building, with the exception of one. The inside of the building looked like a high-tech center in the sky. We expected to see the Senior Technology Leader of the Top of the Universe at any moment.

As we walked through the building, we saw a hallway that led to a giant library. The library was the size of a stadium. It had columns along the walls and down the center of it. There were rows and rows of shelves that were full of books. Some of the books appeared to be ancient because of the cracked leather and fading gold lettering on the bindings. Some of the books appeared to be newer. As far as our eyes could see, there were glowing portals at the end of each row.

At last, we passed through the final corridor of a one-way, glass hallway. We arrived in front of an enormous room with a significant sign that read "The Archives." Unlike the rest of the building, "The Archives" room had bright, sturdy white walls . . . glass. The room was spotless and empty, like a bowl of white milk. Four comfortable, ultra-modern, black, leather, and sterling silver chairs popped up out of the floor. And this was where the action and the real story began…

No sooner had the chairs popped up through the clear floor then a giant movie screen dropped down from the ceiling. I mean really big! In fact, it was enormous. A deep, ancient-sounding man's voice spoke to us. He spoke in English, and the voice came through the overhead speakers. The voice sounded excited and delighted.

He announced, "You have been invited here to help us alter the future."

The four of us thought to ourselves; we *didn't get an invitation to come here.*

He must *not* have been able to read our thoughts or see our faces because, if he had, he would have noticed that we were looking at each other like he was crazy. But he wasn't crazy. Before we could think another thought, he spoke with a stern but inviting voice.

"Let's be clear," he said. "You didn't arrive on the Top of the Universe by yourselves. There were many factors that led you here. The real question before you is this: are you ready to learn your purpose? And in case you weren't aware - and I'm pretty certain you weren't - there is a pre-planned path for each of your lives. Behind the walls in the big library next door, you'll find a book on each of your lives."

Our narrator continued.

"Did you know that your entire future was written in advance, and there are books that have exactly what you are supposed to do in life?"

His last words really got *all* of our attention. We couldn't deny that we had not arrived here by coincidence. An unexpected gift of a telescope drew us to a singing and dancing teenage girl on Mars.

Then the next thing we knew, we were *on* Mars . . . then Neptune, and then Saturn. Then we finally arrived at one of the most spectacular places, and it was in an unknown galaxy.

This was supposed to be just a video game, but it is clearly more than a game. Things appear to be working together for us or against us. I feel like we were mysteriously pulled here. Was it Mr. Matthews' brother? Was it our unsuspecting tour guide, Serapha? Was it just a game? This was definitely a different world.

The narrator heard my thoughts.

"It *is* more than just a game," he said. "We want you to open your books and allow yourselves to see what should be. It's still your choice. Once the contents of your books are revealed to you, you will have a better understanding of who you are, why you were born, and your desires, likes, and even your dislikes.

"There is something special about each one of you . . . and everyone on Earth, for that matter. Everyone is born with gifts and talents that can help them carry out their purpose and destiny. That destiny can be found in their books.

"There's something else you need to be aware of. There are special messengers assigned to you on Earth. There's more time for that conversation later. Right now, we need to first show you your purpose and destiny. Are you ready?"

We all looked at each other and, at the same time, said, "We're ready to go!"

A film began to roll across the screen. The film was a presentation of the world being in a state of chaos, a state of malfunction, or, to put it bluntly, things were falling apart. It wasn't looking good for Earth.

The first film was titled "Chaos." It started out with cars breaking down and airplanes and spacecraft coming to a standstill. The film became worse with every scene. In one scene, kids were being served dirty water while, in another scene, someone in a white lab jacket was trying to treat the pollution levels of Earth's water.

In another scene, people were standing in long lines waiting to get into hospitals. There was a shortage of doctors, nurses, and medical staff. People were holding cell phones that were not working. In still another scene, kids were frustrated because they were trying to play video games that were malfunctioning and breaking down. Airplanes couldn't take off at airports. These scenes continued rolling one after the other. Problems, crises, and disasters were happening all at the same time all over the Earth.

Then a man's voice announced, "It's the year 2040. Earth has a shortage of adults with knowledge of science. Civilization is regressing and standing still. Not enough kids and teenagers thought science was important to life; therefore, the Earth, as we know it, is slowing down. There are not enough people with the necessary knowledge to turn civilization around. It will take at least ten years for a new generation to come along and help."

155

After the narrator finished speaking, the most unusual thing happened. A scene appeared on the screen that had a whole different level of chaos. Firefighters, city officials, and even police officers were knocking on the doors of senior citizens who were eighty and ninety years of age. They were trying to get the seniors to come back to work.

In the scene that followed, two young adults, a man, and a woman, got out of a late model, red sports car and walked over to a near-perfect, green golf course. In a state of panic, they went directly toward a 75-year-old couple that was playing golf. They interrupted their golf game like it was an emergency.

The young adults asked, "Is it possible for you to come back to work for a while? We're having problems figuring things out."

The older man looked at them and hollered, "No! You half-baked kids."

But with compassion, his wife looked at the kids and then looked at her husband and said, "That's cruel."

Her husband replied, "Cruel is what they did to society. They're bums!"

"You're being mean," said the wife.

"Things are going downhill fast!" said the two young adults.

In the next scene, the ultimate thing happens. Some Crossings High School kids showed up at our science teacher, Mr. Matthews', home knocking frantically on his door and begging him to give them another chance to learn science. In the group of kids that showed up at his house were two kids who never turned in their homework. That was rare for Mr. Matthew's class. When the rapid, hard knocks came on his front door, he looked out the window and saw the two boys.

One of the two students pleaded, "Mr. Matthews, we're not playing anymore. We are ready to learn. We really need your help."

Mr. Matthews opened the door and looked at the students, and said, "I'm sorry. I can't help right now. I'm very busy. Let's set up some catch-up assignments next week after school."

He calmly closed the door in their faces. Then he walked into his family room, shaking his head with disappointment. He then sat down and started playing his favorite video game.

Looking at the controller, Mr. Matthews said, "You just can't get around science. I think I'll give them another chance."

Suddenly the screen went black. Then we heard the narrator's voice speak again.

"Please. We need you to carry a message back to Earth about the importance of science." Then the narrator said, "Take another look here."

This time the faces in the movie were familiar. The faces were Madison, Austin, Gabe, and me, as adults. In the first scene, Madison is a research scientist in a laboratory. She was wearing a long, white jacket, and she was working on cancer cures for children and adults.

157

The next scene was in a hospital. Young children were in hospital beds. They were bald. They looked like they might have been cancer patients. In the first hospital scene, the children were sad. In the second hospital scene, the children were happy. They were happy because Madison helped them get well.

Next was Gabe. Gabe, who always liked fast things, walked into a large Boeing 777 aircraft. He was dressed in a pilot's uniform, complete with a captain's cap on his head, the whole nine yards. He was the plane's left-seat pilot. He climbed into the cockpit, checked the instruments, and prepared for takeoff. As the aircraft took off, Gabe had a big smile on his face. In the next scene, Gabe's plane was flying across the Pacific Ocean. In Gabe's final scene, he was instructing younger pilots. There were about twenty-five student pilots in a major airline training room, and Gabe was giving them flight instructions.

Austin's life scene was next. His scene started in a corporate boardroom. Just like I always thought, Austin was an engineer turned executive. And there he was at the head of the boardroom table. He was the president of a high-tech computer security company that protected the U.S. government's computers from hackers. His duty was to protect the country's government secrets from foreign spies and terrorists. His company had just averted another country's attempt to blow up the world with a nuclear bomb. The scene that followed showed the president of the United States congratulating

Austin and his team of scientists. The president was not only talking to Austin, but he was shaking Austin's hand.

Austin smiled back at the president and said, "Thank you, sir."

Now for me. I was a teacher like Mr. Matthews. I was a science professor and also a scientist at a large university. I wore cool, black-rimmed glasses and soft, leather, designer loafers, and my hair was gelled back. The screen showed me lecturing to about 100 college students in the university's auditorium.

Some of the students in my class were studying microbiology for different professions. Some were future engineers, teachers, and environmentalists who wanted to help protect Earth, and others were nurses who wanted to help people. In addition to teaching university students, I was also a scientist with my own lab, where my team and I were researching plant seeds that could be used for medicine. Although I was only in my twenties, I had two laboratories with over twelve people who were working on two different research projects. One project was alternative energy sources for gas. The other project focused on alternative medicine.

On the Top of the Universe and away from Earth, we gained a different perspective about life and science. When the last film scene ended, the four of us were quiet for a long moment, in deep reflection, thinking about what we had just seen.

Austin was the first one to say something.

"That was cool. I met the president. I saved the country, and he congratulated me for it. He shook my hand."

Madison was next.

As if she was still surprised and overwhelmed at the unlimited possibility of the good works that her life could contribute, she said, "I'm going to help people. Me."

Gabe just sat smiling, like his dream had finally come true. We waited for a response from him. He just kept smiling, like it was already done.

Then finally, he said, "That's right. That's me."

Once the presentation of our books' good works was over, and the giant screen was dark, Serapha looked at us.

She said, "That was just a picture frame of what's been prepared for you. You have to step into the picture frame and grow into it. You can't step into the picture frame here, though. You have to go back to Earth and step into the picture frame there. However, before you go, I have another screen to show you."

The narrator began.

"This is what you *don't* want to happen."

The giant screen lit back up, and the next scene was very brief. It showed me going back to Crossings High School as an adult looking in on Mr. Matthews' science class. I was sitting in the back of the class, still admiring Mr. Matthews as he taught his science class.

The next scene showed Madison at a hospital working as a volunteer with sick children who were cancer patients. Madison and the sick children were playing with puppets. One little girl was wheeled into the playroom just to say hi to Madison.

When the nurse wheeled the child into the playroom, she said, "Hello, Madison. Sophia is not feeling well today. She can't play, but she wanted to tell you hi."

The little girl lifted her weak hand slowly and waved to Madison. Then the nurse rolled her wheelchair out of the room. Madison's face became sad as she watched the nurse wheel the sick girl out of the room.

With deep disappointment and sadness in her voice, Madison said, "I wish I could do more for her."

Gabe's scene was a complete reversal of his other one... Instead of flying aircraft, he was standing outside an airport watching large aircraft take off and land. He had become an airplane freak. Another scene showed a picture of Gabe's home. Inside his home were pictures of airplanes everywhere. There were pictures of airplanes in every room of the house. In one room, there were seven model airplanes sitting on a work table. Gabe spent the rest of his life just watching airplanes and building model airplanes.

I had to say that the next scene was very serious . . . but still kind of funny . . . if you had a sense of humor. In the very next scene,

Austin was playing a video game and then stopped playing the game to switch to the evening television news.

The male newscaster reported, "The United States Central Intelligence Agency's computers were hacked and compromised by foreign spies today. The extent of damages is still being evaluated."

While the newscaster was still on the air, someone walked up to the news desk and handed him a note. He stopped speaking to his live audience.

Then he said, "Excuse me for a moment."

He silently read the note. Still on the air, a worried look came over his entire face.

In a serious, solemn tone, the newscaster reported, "We don't know what to expect next." All at once a loud explosion and sirens filled the airwaves and the streets.

Suddenly, the newscaster jumped up and hollered, "I got to go. Take cover!"

And he ran off the set. The television screen went blank. Austin just stood there and looked at the blank television screen like he was hypnotized.

With much regret, Austin shook his head and said, "This should have never happened. I had the ability to change things."

The scene ended. The narrator's voice didn't return, and the short film was over. The large drop-down movie screen was dark again, and there was silence in the room for a moment. A very long moment.

After Serapha *showed us the worlds to come,* she looked directly at us and said in a sincere, serious voice, "Science really matters. It's important that you take science seriously and learn to apply it to your lives. Your lives really matter. You can make a difference."

Following Serapha's last words, the narrator returned and said, "There's more beyond this story. Serapha will tell you more about the messengers and agents you have on Earth."

Serapha began."You are not alone. You have messengers assigned to you on Earth. I'm one of them. Everyone gets a messenger when they are born. I think you call them angels. It's the job of angels to help you step by step to fulfill your destiny. Your purpose and destiny are written in your books in the library. Each of you has a book with your name on it. My job is to help you carry out what is written in your book of life, if you are willing, and help you stay on track. There will be obstacles, but that's where I come into play.

"Most human beings on Earth never complete their purpose and destiny. They don't pay attention to what is on the inside of them. Here's a key, your gifts, talents, and desires are your roadmap to your path, purpose, and destiny.

"Most of the time, my kind is invisible on Earth. "So, how are we able to cooperate with you?" "Well, we read your books before we are assigned to you on Earth. Your book of life is our agenda. It's a roadmap.

"Most people don't know how to cooperate with us, but you have learned just by playing the game on Mars, Neptune, Saturn, and the Top of the Universe.

"The game was a little extreme. Nonetheless, we responded to your words. You were pretty impressed with Saturn using the words' nocturnal animals'. We are always looking for good words, words of light, and words of truth; words to turn things around and move things in the right direction.

"The Top of the Universe is our home. It's a planet full of Light. We are from the Light. We were created to do good works on the Earth and push back the darkness. Your journey has just begun."

CHAPTER 15

Reinforcements

Serapha was only two steps away from us, and she was studying our faces.

"This is it," she said. "I've given you the blueprints for your life. It's up to you to follow them or choose not to follow them. Choosing to follow will be the easiest route for you because this is what you were created to do. You have free will, so you don't have to follow them. However, if you do, you'll be glad. You will make a lot of other people happy, too."

Madison replied, "Will we ever see you again?"

All of us waited for her answer.

"Only if and when you need me. I am called the Helper. I'll be watching your steps."

All four of us seemed relieved by her answer. It wasn't that we felt we couldn't accomplish our goals and the blueprints without her, but it was just that she was our connector. She was wise and full of fun, too. Serapha had become our friend, the kind of friend you would always treasure.

Sadness and regret sank into our re-created, Earthly minds. We couldn't help but be sad because the end of our journey and adventure with Serapha was at hand.

"Oh, there's one other thing I need to share with you," Serapha said. "It's about the Top of the Universe's time clock. Our time moves forward. So when you get back home, it will be the same time that it was when you left. No one will have missed you. It's time to go now."

Before we could say goodbye, Serapha vanished again. After that, we vanished, too.

We were back in the luxury spacecraft with the same flight attendants and pilots. The window shades were up. Through the windows, we could see thousands upon thousands of stars. The stars at the Top of the Universe were spectacular and marvelous. The view outside our windows looked like a dream. Our entire trip was like a dream.

If Serapha was right, we had just visited, vacationed, and fulfilled an appointment on the Top of the Universe. Now we were on our way back to planet Earth.

There are billions of galaxies in the universe, most of them billions of miles from Earth. As we traveled back to Earth, we saw some of them. There were different galaxies with different shapes. Some were spiral-shaped. Some were irregular, and some were egg-shaped.

I saw what appeared to be a galaxy that was flat and round, sort of like a pancake.

Before I could make a comment, Gabe said, "Look! There's the Andromeda Galaxy."

Then I remembered that the Andromeda Galaxy was flat or disk-shaped, like a pancake, and shaped the same as the Milky Way.

As we were flying, things appeared to be going well, and they were until we received a startling alarm from our pilot. The pilot's voice made an unexpected announcement over the intercom.

"We are experiencing troubling turbulence from an unidentified source."

I thought I heard trembling in his voice.

Within a few minutes, he said, "Prepare for a dangerous encounter."

He was trying to sound calm, but nothing about a dangerous encounter is calm.

I couldn't take the suspense of not knowing what was going to happen next, so I pulled the shade up to see what we were really facing.

As I looked through the window, out into the dark universe, I saw swarms of black, warrior-like monster-size dragonflies. The swarms of dragonflies looked like a huge vapor of black smoke, and their grimaced faces gave the impression of warriors who had come to do battle.

As I moved closer to the window to study them, one of them rushed right up to my window and made eye contact with me. Its red, flaming, enormous eyes were set in a black, bubble-shaped head as it stared at me. Then suddenly, it released a stream of frightening-orange fire towards my window. The sight of its malicious eyes and the streaming fire paralyzed me with fear. Its larger-than-life, man-sized body was overwhelming, too.

The swarms of dragonflies, with their two pairs of strong wings and their long bodies, kept pace with our spacecraft as it traveled through the galaxy. They were shadowing us. Madison and I noticed that the spacecraft's speed had been suddenly reduced, too, and the demonic-looking dragonflies had surrounded it.

Although I was frightened beyond belief, I kept my shade slightly open so that I could keep an eye on their actions. It was better to *see* what they were doing than to *imagine* it. I had no idea what was behind their unceasing, hissing sounds and their banging and thumping up against the spacecraft. Then the pilot's voice came across the intercom again, real cool this time, though, like a radio or television announcer.

"We are in a dangerous predicament," he announced. "I believe they are trying to enter the spacecraft and take it over."

This guy had to be an actor or just brave. He should have been jumping out of his skin.

Austin looked at all of us and said in a very serious tone, "Did you hear that? And did you hear how he sounded like an actor reading a script? No emotion or concern."

"Oh. You can believe he's spooked," said Gabe. "He's just trying to keep everyone calm."

"Well," said Austin. "It's too late for that. And to think that we just left a planet full of promises and dreams."

With a worried look on his face, Gabe continued.

"I thought this was a dream flight or dream spacecraft. Did the dreaming end when we left the planet of Light? Are we getting smacked on our way back to Earth?" Nothing had prepared us for this.

I've heard different people say that life and death are in the power of your words. That's something that we have been learning all throughout this journey. Serapha also told us that the messengers respond to our words as well. Well... this was a time we didn't know what to say, but I knew I had to say something.

"These creatures aren't from the Top of the Universe. There is too much gloom in them. I don't even think they're a part of the game or part of the plan."

Just as I was about to have a meltdown, Austin's mind started humming." There has to be a plan of action for unexpected circumstances," he said.

All we saw outside were flames of fire and a black mist coming from the bodies of the dragonflies. *Why couldn't we have made it home without any drama?* I thought.

I remembered reading once about a place called "The Second Heavens in the Circuits of Space." The reading said it was a fictional place. It was supposed to be a place where warfare took place between the Light Forces and Dark Forces of the spirit world. I felt that our spacecraft might have mistakenly drifted right into the middle of their conflict. If that were true, then the spacecraft had a chance to survive the attack because it was just passing through.

In the meantime, I was trying to figure out if this was a potential hijacking or an extra-terrestrial, territorial challenge. Because of the thumping and bumping of the dragonflies against the spacecraft, the spacecraft was rocked back and forth, like a pair of sneakers in a dryer. My mind was racing. I was trying to figure out what was next.

In a terrified voice, Austin shouted, "Oh no!! The door of the spacecraft was just unfastened."

All we could do was wait for the next sequence of actions. We sat frozen with fear. No one said another word, not even Madison. From the direction of the spacecraft door, we could hear steps and hissing sounds moving toward us. The captain, co-pilot, and attendants were no longer in charge. After the door to the spacecraft was opened, the flight attendants sat down real fast behind us, like elementary students running to their seats. The pilots gently closed the door of the cockpit without a sound. They had a good reason to shut the door, and the flight attendants had a good reason to hide behind us.

An extremely tall, slender dragonfly whose face was made up of dark vapors and gold, fiery eyes stood right in front of us. It had an intense look on its face. The dragonfly studied each one of us, one after the other. Its eyes pierced through our very beings. If it was looking for fear, it got a cup running over from us. The fly should have noticed we were innocent, and read that we weren't a threat.

A second dragonfly entered the cabin. It looked just like the first one. Together they produced a veil of darkness over the cabin. It didn't feel like any good would come from this encounter.

Austin nudged me and whispered, "They're heading toward the cockpit."

I looked up toward the ceiling and noticed that, while the pilots were locked in the cockpit, they had opened the glass skylights so that we could see outside the spacecraft. It was a scary sight. The never-ending swarms of vicious dragonflies were above the space-craft, too. There was no getting around it. We were surrounded and had been captured.

Did the pilots really think they would be safe by locking them-selves inside the cockpit? The intruders looked at the locked door and just busted it in with sheer brute force. There was silence in the cockpit. No one came out.

My imagination started to run wild. I started imagining the dragonflies snuffing out the pilots' brains and insides and leaving empty, hollow bodies lying on the floor. At that moment, in the midst of my horrid imaginings, the captain and co-pilot walked through the cockpit door, escorted like prisoners of war by the two enormous dragonflies hovering over them. The larger-than-life insects shoved them in our direction. Although there was room for them to sit in front with us, both of them scrambled into the seats behind us. We all sat there frozen. The dragonflies then walked away, leaving us unattended.

I was uncertain how far away the flies were, so I whispered to Gabe.

"What would you call this? A game or a solar trip? Actually, *trip* is a better word."

"Until we actually make it home," he whispered back, "I'm not certain. That is *if* we make it back home."

Then in a hopeless-sounding voice, he said, "We don't have any choice but to hope for the best."

Even though he was trying to be positive, I could tell he was going down. I tried to encourage him.

"Watch your thoughts and your words," I reminded him. "We are in space. Remember that in space, words have a lot more power than on Earth. Things happen faster out here, too."

Gabe and Madison looked like they were about to kiss life good-bye. I had to say something to encourage them, too. "We didn't come this far to get cut off. We didn't come out here into space to get lost, either. And we weren't granted a trip to the Top of the Universe to see our destiny and purpose for them never to come to pass.

"The dragonflies are not a part of our world or our story. They showed up to steal, kill, and destroy. Remember the Hosts. The Hosts are for the children of men. We weren't told that they wouldn't help Earth youth in outer space. Maybe there is another group of Hosts for youth traveling in space."

I was trying to encourage them, but the more I talked, the more I realized that I needed someone to encourage *me*.

This whole attack didn't make any sense. Why would dark forces attack us after we just left the planet of light? They had to see the light that was on us. We could even see the light on each other, although it seemed quite natural now. They appeared to be intelligent beings. I believe they knew that our spacecraft had come from the Top of the Universe.

Madison finally opened her mouth and said, "I think the dragon-flies are trying to cut our lives off. They don't want us to fulfill the purpose for our lives. The culprits are more than just haters. They are destroyers . . . to steal our existence, and to deprive Earth from the good we can do."

"Madison, I think you're right," I said. "Look. We have a choice before us. We can focus on the negative or on the positive. It's not written that the dragonflies are going to kill us. Our instincts, knowledge, and words still have power. We saw the power of our words at work on Mars, Neptune, and Saturn. More important . . . we learned our purpose, destiny, and the books of life on the Top of the Universe."

"I believe our purpose and destiny have more power than these despicable harmful creatures' possible intentions toward us," Austin added. Then he just looked at us like we were supposed to follow along.

While the dragonflies were secretly communicating with each other in the front of the spacecraft, I quietly shared my thoughts with my friends.

"Do you think our purpose is strong enough to keep us alive and get us back home?"

The four of us considered once again what we had discovered on the Top of the Universe. After a few minutes of soul searching, Gabe said, "It doesn't matter if we are a pilot, a teacher, an artist, a doctor, researcher, engineer, nurse, musician, or business person ... whatever... as long as we do what was in our books. That's what is important.

"Serapha showed up and reacted to our words, but her ultimate goal was to show us our purpose. She showed up to help us carry it out."

"The power is in the purpose," Austin said. "You can't kill purpose."

Without anybody saying another word, the atmosphere shifted from fear to calm. We were no longer afraid of the dragonflies that hovered over our young lives. Soon after the atmosphere changed, we heard continuous, low, roaring wind sounds approaching the spacecraft. As the unfading sounds moved closer, they sounded like a whooshing of air, and it kept getting louder every moment.

The dragonflies started looking around the spacecraft. I looked outside my window and caught sight of a mighty, warrior-like celestial being descending from space toward the spacecraft. He was clothed in silver armor. His face was brown with sharp facial features.

Suddenly another celestial warrior flew toward the spacecraft. Then a third one trailed him. It was a fantastic sight in the sky, and I was relieved. A host of hundreds of mighty, celestial warriors were approaching us. The brown-faced warriors, clothed in pure light, rushed toward the dragonflies.

The dragonflies went on the defense, and the battle was on! Flashes of light and dark bars of light were swinging through the dark sky. As the conflict intensified, the skies sparkled with light-filled weapons and flashes of light. It looked like the Fourth of July fire-works. We didn't know *what* to make of the display before our eyes. What I really mean is we couldn't tell who was winning or losing.

The dragonflies that had surrounded the spacecraft turned their attention from us. They were focused completely on what was happening in the skies around them. One by one, they became engaged in combat with the celestial warriors that had just arrived.

The Hosts of Light, the celestial warriors, continued to appear and increase in number. Through the brightness of the shining stars, we saw slices of translucent bars falling and floating in space. It wasn't long before I realized the warriors of light were dissecting their bodies as they fought. That's why they kept increasing in number. I didn't feel bad about it.

Some of the dragonflies turned back. Others vanished. And still, others turned into red vapors. I thought we were going to be rescued from the intruders that were inside the spacecraft's cabin. Instead, they turned into red vapors and vanished before our eyes.

After the swift withdrawal and disappearance of the dragonflies, the glowing brown warriors whirled around and around the space-craft. Their whirling manner was so relaxed that it seemed as if they were taking a break before their next assignment. We marveled at their grand appearance and were thrilled beyond words by their heroic rescue.

As the striking warriors lingered outside the now terror-free spacecraft, Austin was the first one to speak.

"I sure wish they would come inside!" he said enthusiastically. "I would love to meet them. I've never met real-life, honest-to-goodness warriors before."

Apparently, it wasn't meant to be. The Hosts of Light, the magnificent celestial warriors, departed as swiftly as they came. We were all disappointed that we didn't get to meet them, but the disappointment didn't last long.

Wouldn't you know it? Serapha, in her typical galaxy-girl fashion, appeared and flew through the walls of the spacecraft like they were thin sheets of paper. She stood before us with a commanding presence. She stood there for a long moment, looking at each of us individually and nodding. Then she spoke. "Now, no one hinders you. Your path is clear. Continue on . . ."

Before she disappeared again, Madison rushed to ask the question we all wanted to know the answer to.

"Who were the good, glowing, brown male and female warriors that rescued us?"

"They are the Special Forces or the Destiny Enforcers," Serapha explained.

"Will we ever see them again?"

"You probably never will *see* them," answered Serapha, "but they will always be there to enforce your destiny when you start walking toward it ... no matter how small the steps."

We would have preferred for Serapha to stay longer, but she departed right away, and we continued our journey toward Earth.

There were other unanswered questions. For one, I really wanted to know more about the dragonflies. Mainly, will we run into them on Earth? Why did they come after us? They studied us for a long time. I felt like they could read our thoughts. Do they know about our books? Do they know about our school?

We experienced a supernatural dimension . . . beyond the world we knew. Serapha, the Reinforcers, and the dragonflies had some things in common. They had the ability to appear, disappear, transport, and transform themselves. *Are they all aliens, extra-terrestrials, spirit beings, or angels? What?*

If Serapha came to influence lives on Earth, then the dragonflies were probably coming to Earth to influence lives, too. But in the wrong way. Where did they come from, anyway? Perhaps they descended from another planet. Maybe they live above Earth's atmosphere. Wouldn't it be wild if they came from the inside of the Earth's core? They could have escaped from hell, wherever that is. And if there *is* a hell, let's just hope that there's a heaven with its own host of beings.

CHAPTER 16

Watchmen

Rumble, rumble, rumble! My body was bouncing against an unfamiliar, enclosed surface and was hitting it back and forth like I was the little silver ball in a pinball game. Yet I was moving forward like a rocket shooting through space. *We were being transported again!* The "Solar System Stretch" game had transported us once again.

We arrived in a white, radiant portal that stood still, like a waiting room. There were walls, but there were no chairs. Unlike the tumbling, tunnel-like portal that transported us to the ocean or the spinning portal that spilled us onto Mars, this portal was somewhat level. We weren't moving, either. It felt like we were in limbo. As our eyes adjusted to the glowing room, we heard faint sounds coming from a distance. Sounds of voices and music playing.

"Are those voices coming from Earth?" Austin asked. "That sounds like Justin Bieber singing and the voices sound like teenagers. Someone is communicating with Earth, or Earth is communicating with someone. I don't think we are stuck in this zone. Hearing songs and those voices have to mean something."

"It's a sign of some sort," I responded. "I believe the game is signaling us to come to a destination. The destination has something to do with Earth."

"If they are listening to Justin Bieber, they probably are teenagers . . . or younger," Austin replied. "We can't stay here forever. Let's push the controllers and see if they will take us to where the voices are coming from. Maybe we have a say in this part of the game."

We all pushed the controllers at the same time and arrived in a new destination. We were full of questions and surprises. From the appearance of things, we had entered a large, contemporary, office-like lobby with a glass ceiling. Through the lobby's glass ceiling, we could see spectacular stars spreading like a rope across the universe's sky. The stars were brighter and larger than any stars I had ever witnessed, with the exception of the Sun. The stars were so close that they created daylight in the building. Because of the brilliant light, I wasn't certain if we had arrived during the evening or the day. I knew one thing for sure; this didn't feel like the doorsteps of Earth.

To our surprise, the lobby's walls were covered with colorful, cheerful images of teenagers like us. Austin asked us a puzzling question that he knew we didn't have the answer to. He just said out loud what we were all wondering.

"Why are there so many teenage faces on the walls? The faces appear to be from Earth. Imagine that. Look. Their faces are Asian, African, Spanish, and even European!"

With an air of doubt, Gabe said, "What makes you think they are from Earth? We don't even know where *we* are, why we are here, and who they really are."

"Gabe, I see your point," I said. "Austin, I see your point, too. However, it is still odd that over a hundred plate-sized youth snapshots are greeting us. You think? Where's the storyline? Here it comes! Shoot, they are tall!"

While we were examining the faces on the walls, two super tall teenagers, well over seven feet tall, a male and a female, walked into the lobby. The male had chestnut brown skin that glowed like lightning. He had a chiseled, lean body and a strong, noble-looking face. The female was a glowing, coffee cream color, slender, and very shapely. I would say that she was cute! Fascinating... their bodies were semi-transparent. Imagine that!

Before we could take a second look or say anything, the striking and noble-looking male teenager reached out and greeted us in a warm, strong voice.

"Welcome. I am Malik, and this is Tien."

His female companion didn't say a word. The girl was very observant as she smiled with her almond-shaped eyes.

With an air of confidence and authority, Malik looked at us pointedly and asked, "Would you mind following us?"

We glanced at each other to make certain we were in agreement. We were, so we all nodded our heads.

Then Austin spoke up quickly and said, "Yes, we'll follow you."

We followed them without hesitation. It was an easy decision. The situation felt like fate.

Our greeters didn't waste any time as they ushered us through the wide, white, silent halls of the one-story building. As we walked through the building, we continued to see the dramatic, eye-catching stars through the glass ceiling. The seemingly low, shining stars reminded us that we were no longer on Earth.

When we walked down the last hallway and turned the final corner, an open control room stood right before us. The open room was lined with large wall monitors, and there were medium-sized monitors stationed at desks with attendants. There had to be at least a hundred monitors attended by about a hundred super-tall teenagers. The attendant teenagers looked like our greeters, except their skin tones were multiple shades, and they all had different features. The teenagers' skin shades varied from brown to white, even blue... but all of them had a radiant glow.

Austin slightly bent his head down and whispered loud enough for only the four of us to hear.

"You can see through all their bodies. There's nothing inside. Go figure that. Not an Earth body!"

The room full of monitors caught our eye, but the teenagers, that were just about every color of the rainbow, captured our attention even more.

"Wow! Reminds me of Skittles," Austin said. "There are lime-green, ocean-blue, and even violet bodies in front of those monitors and standing all around. They kind of look like the girl from Mars, Serapha."

The males' bodies were like Malik's, lean and chiseled, and the females were shapely, similar to Earth women in different shapes.

I wasn't surprised when Gabe looked at Austin and me and re-marked, "Check out those bodies."

Gabe's mind was in a spin again.

Our greeters hadn't invited us into the control room. We were still standing in the entrance and unable to see the images on the revolving monitor screens. The screen images really didn't matter yet, because we were still trying to process the rainbow people.

Gabe looked directly at Malik and said, "This looks like a control room in an airport."

"It *is* a control room," Malik answered, "but we are not dispatching planes. We're dispatching something higher."

"Look. The teenage attendants are vanishing one by one right before our eyes. As soon as one departs, another one returns," Madison said.

Like a rotating movie, new images continued to pop up on the screens throughout the host station. The images reminded me of some struggles and challenges that teenagers on Earth face. There were monitors with teens experiencing all kinds of challenges: painful anxiety and depression, unnecessary and heartless bullying, loneliness in a world full of people, rejection without understanding, sickness, and disease in a world full of medicine, abandonment in the midst of love, drug abuse, and lack of purpose and destiny in a world of prom-ise.

As we looked into a screen to the right of us, we saw a series of images that caught and held our attention immediately.

Malik explained what we were looking at.

"We are dispatching people to help the youth on Earth. The monitors help us find our assignments. Through monitors, we listen and watch youth affairs, events, and circumstances that pop up throughout the Earth."

Before Malik could finish his sentence, in a low but strong tone, Austin said, "I told you. This is about Earth kids."

"We are a small universal host," Malik continued. "Our host does its best to listen and intervene in the lives of youth. We don't get every case, but we attend to the cases that reach us."

"Exactly what do you do?" asked Madison.

"We guard, protect, encourage, guide, rescue, and more. We are helpers," Malik answered.

"How do you know when to help?"

Malik gladly answered her question and remarked, "Our Host listens and responds to words within the monitors. We hear calls for help and hope, and we come. There are always challenges. There are always struggles. And there is always help, too."

"So, you are like ambulances, with the exception that there are no sirens or delays."

"That's it. It's about words and listening. On Earth words have power. Words aren't just used to communicate. They are used to move things. It happens all the time, even when you don't notice it. In worlds outside of Earth and within the universe, words are used with skill because we understand the power of them more. Here, words are like technology. They work for us and move things."

"I never heard about you on Earth," Austin said.

"There's a lot going on, both on Earth and outside of Earth, that you not aware of," Malik continued. "The teenage hosts are not the only invisible agents going in and out of Earth and around the universe. There are good hosts and bad hosts. Sometimes we appear on Earth as a flash of light when we carry out our assignments. We operate as invisible good agents."

Perhaps it was fate when the next fierce-looking host received the next screen's notice. She was a girl. We didn't need anyone to tell us that, but Madison did. Madison was thrown off by the color of her skin. The female host just stood there with her back toward us, looking at the screen. We weren't close to the screen, so it was difficult to see what caught her eye. Besides, the screen was kind of dark. We moved in a little closer so we could see more.

On the screen, a full moon was sitting in place over a clear midnight sky. Below the sky was a dock full of small and midsized boats. They weren't moving and seemed to be empty. Then a cargo ship pulled into the end of the dock. With the exception of the full moon in the midnight sky, there were little to no visible lights around the ships or warehouse buildings positioned in front of the dock. We were all standing still, staring at a motionless screen.

In sudden alarm, Madison said, "What's going on? What's that?"

In somewhat of a stupor, I said, "Huh!"

'Quiet,' Madison murmured, "Let's move closer."

We moved closer to the monitor's screen and stood right behind Madison. At first, we had difficulty distinguishing what was taking place. Madison and the female teenage host caught on first.

We just stood there in disbelief at what we watched taking place. As our eyes pierced through the darkness, we saw what appeared to be two men leading a group of young girls, between twelve and sixteen years old off a ship, one by one. It was far from normal. It became worse by the moment. The girls were blindfolded and holding hands in a line.

In a single line, the two men ushered them toward what looked like a warehouse with painted windows. The girls were lined up like prisoners.

The men didn't look back. They just kept moving forward with the line. Right before they entered the building, the men turned on flashlights that cast light through the entrance and down a hallway that led to an open room.

In a worried whisper, Madison asked, "Are the girls hopeless? They are making them walk in the dark." No one said a word.

Then a deep rough voice came from the screen and hollered, "Move!"

In the darkness, it was difficult to see an image. My heart just sank.

When Madison finally pulled her eyes from the screen, she glanced at the teenage host and whispered to us, "Look at her eyes. That's the first time I've witnessed compassion and fierceness together."

I took a second look and said, "Madison, lions, and lambs don't go together. She is furious."

Malik overheard our conversation and, without whispering, said, "They call her the Burning One."

Right before our eyes, the female host vanished, leaving a dark blue mist. I could see why Madison wasn't certain about her being a girl at first. She did have a fierceness about her. After she disappeared, we expected to see her inside the screen, but we didn't. Instead, we saw something like blue shafts of light or blue electrical currents inside the dark warehouse.

The screen was still dark, but we could see outlines of the men and the girls. The next thing we saw looked like volts of electricity surging through the men's bodies. I don't think they had a chance to run. They probably didn't even see it coming. Blue shafts of light were flying rapidly through their bodies like swords.

The blue shafts of lights continued to strike at them. They were slicing through their bodies. For some reason, the men weren't falling to pieces.

"Ahhh! Ahhh! Ahhh!" they screamed.

All we could hear were their piercing cries, full of extreme emotion and pain. At first, there was yelling and screaming. Then there was a horrible howling, like wild wolves. When their bodies were finally exhausted with pain and agony, they plummeted to the ground. After that, we only heard groaning that grew dimmer and dimmer with each moment that passed.

Because our attention was so totally focused on the screens, we hadn't noticed that we were getting warm. The area where we were standing had become hot. We started sweating.

I looked at Austin, Gabe, and Madison and said, "That's pure, raw girl power."

The screen before us was quiet. The last groaning sounds had come and gone. The blindfolded girls weren't certain if their captors were badly injured or dead. Either way, they realized within themselves that the inner darkness of their captors' souls had been weakened to the point of no return. The girls didn't know if the vicious violence had ended or not. There was an intruder in the building, and the silence was deafening.

We were still glued to the screen. We noticed the inside of the warehouse had become lighter and more visible. One of the girls removed her blindfold. Like a brave leader, she removed the next girl's blindfold. Following their brave leader, one by one, the girls began to untie each others' blindfolds. The rest of the girls who were waiting stood still, paranoid and too scared to move, probably still in shock, not knowing whether it was time to be relieved, to cry, or to simply adjust their eyes that had been blindfolded longer than they cared to remember. Another girl noticed a light near the far entrance.

She frantically told the girls, "It's time to escape!"

As a group, they all rushed toward the light and the entrance. While running out, one of the younger girls spotted a cell phone on the ground next to one of the men's bodies. She reached over and grabbed it as she ran, hollering.

"I got a phone! I got a phone!"

The girls ran like they were in a race, close to the finish line. They did not know what was on the other side of the darkness. And I don't think they cared. They were running for their lives. When they reached the entrance, they froze for a moment, probably not certain if there were more captors waiting on the other side of the door.

Suddenly, one girl in the group hollered, "Move!"

At that command, all the girls made their way outside the building.

When they all made it outside the warehouse, there was a pleasant surprise. They were all alone on the dock. The only thing they found were the empty boats and the full moon shining down from the midnight sky.

Taking the last step to liberty, the young girl with the phone walked over to the older girl who had untied her blindfold and handed her the phone. The older girl didn't waste a second. She called 911 immediately. After she dialed the phone's first digit of hope, the screen before us faded slowly and then went dark. Then just as quickly as the fierce female host had vanished, she reappeared in front of us at the host station.

Right after Burning One returned, Malik raised his hand and motioned us to come to one of the large monitors to watch another host in action. On the monitor's screen, two teenage boys were struggling to stay afloat in a lake. They appeared to be drowning.

As the water continued to rush over them, one of the boys hollered, "Help!"

Right after that, the other boy hollered, "Help! I am *not* drowning today."

No one heard them. They weren't far from the shore. It was a shame because the shore was full of people. The teenagers put their best effort forth to wrestle with the water, but their legs and arms were growing weak and tired. The boys would have stopped if they had accepted that the odds were against them. They seemed to be determined to stay alive. The instinct for survival is very strong.

In front of us, a male teenage host stood rocking back and forth like a runner in the blocks at the start of a race. He was poised and ready to spring into action. He was looking directly into the screen where the two teenage boys struggled in the lake. From our standpoint, the odds seemed high that he would jump right through the screen. His hands flew forward in the air, and most of the room turned their heads in his direction.

"I got this!" he announced.

In a second, he vanished into thin air, leaving a deep green mist that was the same color as his skin. He left it circulating where he had stood.

As we continued to watch the screen, two flashes of light appeared around the teens in the water. Out of nowhere, two large objects were dumped right in front of them with a big splash! The boys instinctively grabbed the dark objects with the little strength they had left. What had they grabbed? Whatever it was, their arms were holding it tight and steady.

There wasn't a lot of movement in the water anymore. We realized the dark, round objects were actually sturdy, black tire tubes. At last, they were able to keep their heads above the swirling water. Their bodies, however, were still submerged in waters deeper than they could ever imagine. Although the violent struggle with the lake had ceased, the two were still a long way from being safe.

We heard humming engine sounds breaking rapidly against the waters. A short distance from the struggling boys, we spotted a motorboat. On the screen, sparks of light were racing across the motorboat driver's ear. In a twist of events, the boat's driver immediately received a thought to steer his boat around and fish in another direction. The driver assumed it was his own thought. When he steered his boat in the opposite direction, he spotted the two struggling teenagers and one by one; he pulled them out of the water. The wearied boys climbed aboard the boat in unbelief, amazement, and gratitude.

One of the boys cried, "Someone heard us! This is a miracle!"

In the blink of an eye, the teenage host rushed back and reappeared in the control room in his full skin. The moment that Malik noticed the host helper had returned, he turned toward him and gave him a high five.

"Good job!" he said.

The control room was minus the songs and teenage chatter that drew us to this destination. In its place was the realization that someone really cared about teenagers on Earth.

The pop-up screens had an element of heaviness to them because of the very nature of the distress calls. There were no sad faces or gloomy overcasts in the control room. Instead, it was full of hosts standing at attention like swift, single-minded warriors. For them, it was a race against time, and Earth mattered.

Something about this experience was causing Austin, Madison, Gabe, and me to look inward at ourselves. Austin's eyes were fixed on the Host, and he was in deep thought. Then finally, he spoke.

"I can't get past their eyes," Austin reflected. "It's hard to put in words, but the youths' lives and futures are in their hands and eyes. Can't you see the youths' images reflected in their eyes? Their eyes are like a camera, picking up the images and storing them."

I began to see what Austin saw. He was right about their eyes. They were full of images, compassion, and a call to execute vengeance on calamities, injustices, wrongs, and just plain bad situations aimed against Earth's youth. There was an intense, stirring motion in the room like waves as the Host continued to examine the screens and carry the weight of Earth's youth on their shoulders. In each incident, after the hosts figured out what was happening, they dashed out like lightning to the rescue.

I looked at Malik, Madison, and the team and said, "This is too much for an Earth kid like me to carry. Maybe that's why they had to give the assignment to universal teenagers."

Malik immediately responded to my statement.

"It's not heavy when you fix the problem quickly. It's exhilarating! There's nothing like it. That's why we exist."

His comments were over my head. They made me think about my book again.

Then I said, "For teenagers, your lives have a lot of meaning and purpose." We found a deeper meaning and purpose for our lives in space too. The first half of the screen stories were sad and somewhat troubling, but the end results were satisfying. It was relieving to see the before-and-after pictures. The teenage hosts didn't change the whole universe, but they made life easier and better for those within their reach, even though they were far away in a different world.

I knew our journey with the super-tall teenage hosts had come to an end when Malik walked over to us and spoke.

"We just want you to know that you are not alone. There is someone watching. There is someone that cares, and there is help. Remember that."

I was right. It was the end because, after Malik's last words, we disappeared from his world and turned up in another.

CHAPTER 17

The Turnaround

It wasn't long before we were traveling toward Earth again. This time our eyes were fixed upon a galaxy, we were all familiar with, the Milky Way Galaxy. When we saw the Milky Way, we saw Earth's solar system enclosed within it. Then we knew we were close to home.

It was obvious this was a game because there was no way we could be going this fast on a normal spacecraft. Given the speed of this vehicle, we were expected to arrive in Earth's solar system soon. Neptune was the farthest planet from Earth. We soon passed by it. The thought of Neptune made the four of us all look the other way just to ensure that we never saw that place again.

In the midst of all the excitement that we had experienced, no one was really thinking about Mr. Matthews' twin brother, Mervin . . . except for me. Madison, Austin, and Gabe were still talking about the massive, silver-white horses and how they became expert horsemen for the first time in their lives. No matter how we got around it, this trip was still set in motion by Mr. Matthews' brother, and he would have some answering to do.

As we moved back through Earth's solar system, I counted each planet and its moons. It was definitely an up-close and personal view. I knew this was a once-in-a-lifetime experience, but nothing compared with being back home. And even though the Top of the Universe had been a very special place, it didn't feel like home.

Once again, however, our flight was suddenly interrupted. We didn't understand what had happened. At first, we thought we had arrived home in rocket time. Inwardly, we felt it was too soon, and we were right.

No one noticed that we had actually touched down on an unnamed dwarf planet. The landing was uneventful. Unknowingly to us, our spacecraft was programmed to land on this dwarf planet before reaching Earth. It was all in the game.

The captain informed us that we were in the Milky Way galaxy.

Then he set us at ease by saying, "Don't be alarmed. Things are fine. No more dragonflies or tests and trials. We are making a surprise visit to some Crossings High School students. You might even know them."

Austin just about jumped out of his seat and shouted, "What!?! I bet it's those missing boys. Ahh, shoot!"

"It's unlikely," I responded.

"Likely," Austin said suspiciously.

The captain didn't appear to be alarmed by our conversation about the missing boys.

However, he did change the focus when he said, "A space shuttle will be here any minute to transport us to the center of the planet. Once it arrives, we will move from our spacecraft to the small shuttle."

Somewhat bothered, Austin asked, "Exactly where are we?"

"This is just a small, offbeat planet at the end of the galaxy. We won't be here long," the Captain said.

I could tell Austin wasn't satisfied with the answer. He replied back to the captain."We'll see."

On our other journeys, we didn't have to put on space suits. We should have. Anyway, the captain asked us to put protective, astronaut suits on top of our clothes. Soon after that, an unmarked, eggshell-colored, small space shuttle arrived with a man inside who was suited up in grey, bulky, protective space gear. There was one driver and one other man inside the shuttle. When we took a closer look inside, we noticed that the man was shorter than an average adult. His helmet just about covered his whole face, so we couldn't tell if he was a teenager or an adult.

The small shuttle was designed like a capsule or a cone. We climbed into it. Our spacecraft's pilot didn't come with us, but the co-pilot did. The pilot decided to stay with the spacecraft. It was a good thing that he decided to stay because there was only enough room for Madison, Austin, Gabe, the co-pilot, and myself to fit into the shuttle comfortably.

We closed the door, and the shuttle took off suddenly like a subway train. It traveled along metal tracks. As we traveled across the planet's landscape, the skies' sparkling stars gave us more than enough light to see the planet's dark, grey, flat plains that appeared to go on forever. The ground was dry with open cracks. The atmosphere was still and dreary. From what we could see, the planet looked lifeless. There were no mountains or hills in sight. The four of us were puzzled by the planet's lifeless and motionless setting.

With a suspicious look in his eyes, Austin looked at all three of us and said, "This doesn't look right. The place is deserted."

In agreement, Gabe slowly said, "Where are we going?"

The driver spoke up right away and said, "This planet functions underground."

After the captain's remarks, we were in a wait-and-see kind of mode. On the Top of the Universe, we felt like we had seen it all, but this was a sharp contrast to there. Instead of going up and down on escalators in midair, we headed beneath the planet's surface.

In a matter of seconds, we were completely underground and traveling across the center of the planet as the shuttle's speed increased. The shuttle was still on the same tracks. As it moved swiftly, clinging onto the tracks and making rapid, clicking sounds, we glanced outside the windows and saw bright continuous hallways on the other side of the tracks. The hallways looked like the inside of a subway station. We kept looking, but we didn't see anyone standing in those hallways.

When the shuttle finally stopped moving, and its doors sprang wide open, wouldn't you know it? We were greeted by one of the missing Crossings High School teenagers.

Boy, had he changed! He greeted us like a model citizen.

"Welcome to the International Youth Space Mission! I am glad to see someone from home!"

I don't ever remember this student being friendly or smiling. He had on skinny, black pants; a black turtleneck sweater; and he had a nice haircut. He introduced himself as Christopher. I realized something that was almost overshadowed by the extreme turnaround in Christopher's behavior. He didn't introduce himself to our spacecraft's co-pilot. Only us.

After noticing the big turnaround in Christopher's personality and appearance, through her teeth, Madison mumbled, "This must be 'The City of Hope'." I understood what she was saying. We all did.

Madison was stunned that Christopher and maybe the other missing Crossings students were at the International Youth Space Mission. While Austin and Gabe were talking to Christopher, Madison stepped aside and asked our spacecraft co-pilot a question that I overheard.

"Exactly how did this Crossings High School student get here?"

"Well, first of all, he had to be invited. Secondly, his parents had to agree for him to come. It's a special learning project, and it's for students with potential," he said.

"Potential. Is that what it was?!" Madison said in surprise.

Still amazed by Christopher's new appearance and selection of clothes, Madison just shook her head and looked directly at him, and said, "Must be fate."

Christopher's parents probably felt proud that he was invited. Real-world... they probably wanted a break. They probably saw it as an opportunity, too. How many parents can say their kids went on a space mission? How many parents would send their kids to space? Sometimes people will do anything for a little respect and recognition.

Could this have been connected to the International Space Station? After all, this was another planet. It seems like Austin, Madison, and I would have been invited to participate in a youth space mission. We are good students, and we follow the rules.

Before Madison asked another question, Christopher motioned us to follow him.

"I have lots to show you here," he said, "and we don't have a lot of time."

We followed Christopher on a tour of his ultra-modern mission school. As we walked through the hallways, we glanced through the classroom windows. The classrooms were large, but the class sizes were small. There were about five students in each class. Altogether there were about fifteen classrooms. Interestingly, each classroom had five flags representing five different countries. I saw the American flag.

In surprise, Gabe shouted, "There's my flag! Brazil!"

I recognized the South African flag, too.

"This must mean there are students from both of these countries. I bet the student right in front of the room is from Brazil. He looks just like me," Gabe said. "Students get a lot of help when class sizes are small. I bet that makes them feel special."

Feeling appreciative, Christopher added, "I feel special because I got a second chance. My story has changed. What you saw on Earth was a chapter in my life. I found out that wasn't who I really was. I wasn't born to be a truant, in trouble all the time, and not do well in school. That's not my permanent story."

It meant a lot to Christopher to share his story with people who knew the before-and-after person. He continued sharing.

"Fortunately, someone saw something in me and invited me here. There's a lot more to me than what I thought. To be honest . . . deep inside, I felt and hoped that there had to be more. I don't look the same or talk the same because I am not the same.

"Life is clear in Space. There are no distractions. It's easier for me to focus and concentrate. No anger here. It's strange. I feel comfortable with myself in a way I never felt on Earth. I discovered my talents and creativity. I have something to offer the world."

Austin sized up Christopher's conversation and his experience. He kept looking at him like there was something he wanted to say. Then he said it.

"Did you see your book? Did you see your purpose and destiny?"

Christopher was quiet for a moment, and we understood why.

"Yes. I saw the book that was written about my life. There was a lot more in it than what I saw on Earth." he said.

"Did you see your books?" he asked us.

Madison answered, "We saw our books."

Austin, Gabe, and I just nodded our heads in agreement.

Who thought there were books written about our lives before we lived them?

"I am only here for a while," Christopher said. "My mission is just about accomplished. I am headed back to Earth soon."

Well, Christopher said what we wanted to hear, and we said what he wanted to know. Then like nothing unusual had happened or had been said, we continued our tour through the International Youth Space Mission.

I thought the special Youth Space Mission only focused on space, but I was mistaken. As we continued our tour, I looked through one of the classroom windows and noticed there was an art class going on with students. Then Austin drew our attention to the actual art in the classroom.

"Look at those student drawings," he said. "They are drawing and painting like professional artists. I wonder if those are their natural abilities or if they had re-created minds from the Top of the Universe. If they journeyed out to space this far, they might have stopped by the Top of the Universe. Just saying. Maybe they rode on lightning-fast horses like us, too."

"Hey, let's have one of the students draw a sketch of us all together," Christopher said.

He led us into the class and asked one of the student artists to draw us. Right before our eyes, the student sketched a near-perfect, black-and-white drawing of us. After he finished the drawing, they didn't have to tell me anything else. By the speed of his drawing, I knew his brain and talent had been quickened. I shouldn't have said this out loud, but I did.

"When he goes back home to Earth, his parents will probably think it's their creative genes and be proud."

Gabe responded to my comment and said, "Maybe it was their genes, and the planet just made them speed up and come alive."

Gabe made a good observation about the speed of the artist's ability. He continued.

"The game stimulated our existing abilities, and our books just pulled out of us who we really were and were to become. His parents do have a reason to be proud. It's really him. Something had to be there already."

While Gabe and I were fascinated by the artist and his artwork, Madison took a stroll to another classroom. She was in the choir room. Yes, I said the choir room . . . in space. She was singing her songs and dancing identically to Serapha. And wouldn't you have guessed it... out of nowhere, Serapha appeared again, picked up a mic, and began to sing and dance with Madison.

Austin was right. It was a magnetic pull. We were magnetically pulled to Serapha, and she was magnetically pulled to us. And it didn't start on Mars, nor did it end on the Top of the Universe. Madison and Serapha were singing and dancing in harmony without music as if they had been practicing together forever.

The students in the class were amazed by their dancing abilities as the two of them shifted their bodies to the right and the left, their arms spinning back and forth in the air. Serapha was dancing joyfully just like the first time she appeared to us on Mars through the lens of the telescope.

There were classes for everyone at the International Youth Space Mission. At the same time the dances were happening, Austin slipped away to the software class with the techies.

The classroom looked futuristic, full of witty inventions that we hadn't seen on Earth. Austin was looking over innovative software with a student from India. When we walked into the room and motioned to him that it was time to go, he jotted down a couple of notes and said goodbye to everyone, and joined us in the hallway.

Our space shuttle had returned and was moving close to us. Madison, Austin, and Gabe were looking directly at the approaching shuttle, fully feeling that this was our last stop and we were finally headed home.

Christopher eyed me and said, "Well, it's time to go. I just wanted to let you know. You all are not alone."

Then with a glow and excitement in his eyes, he said, "So . . . how does space feel?"

I paused.

Then I said, "It's hard to put in words. A lot has happened. A whole lot has happened."

Our spacecraft's co-pilot walked toward us in the hall and led us to the shuttle we had arrived on earlier. Christopher walked with us.

Just before we climbed into the shuttle, he looked at us and said, "The future is bright, and we all have hope."

Before he turned around to leave, he smiled genuinely and said, "And help. I got help."

Christopher brought us to a moment of truth. We realized, like him, that we had found hope and help . . . and way out in space, too.

CHAPTER 18

Luminous Ones

Before we knew it, we were off again. This time we really were on our way home. By now, our co-pilot had regained his spacecraft, confidence, and peace of mind. He was streaming in space and time, and I bet the thoughts and imaginations in his mind were journeying, too.

According to Gabe, we hadn't quite reached Earth's galaxy yet, but we were close. As we shot through the universe, the co-pilot was resorting to small talk, but Gabe, the second master of the skies, decided to educate us on the skies. The Archives had really left a mark on him, especially those archives films. The archives confirmed and supported what was already stirring inside of him.

"You know. Right now, we're journeying through the last tail of the Andromeda Galaxy," Gabe said.

With his fingers pointing, he pointed out some things to us.

"See the Milky Way over there. It's a distance. The Andromeda Galaxy is the closest large galaxy next to our galaxy, the Milky Way. We are still a couple million light-years away."

I just looked at Gabe and said, "Really? Wow."

The thought was too astronomical for my mind to grasp. The co-pilot just smiled.

After Gabe finished his space speech, the co-pilot started his small talk again. I could tell he was comfortable with us. When you think about it, we had been through quite a bit together. In the back of my mind, I had this recurring feeling that we weren't the first Earth kids he had met. In fact, I was certain there was a lot more he knew about our trip than what he had shared with us.

Suddenly, something crazy started happening in my mind.

As I held my head, I shouted, "WHAT'S HAPPENING TO ME!? Creative ideas and thoughts are downloading into my head like a computer. They're like flashes of light moving across my mind."

It didn't make sense. If I'd had a paintbrush and a canvas in my hand, I would have started capturing the rushing images and landscapes. If I'd had a pen, I would have written in detail the inventions that were popping into my head.

I looked at Madison, Austin, Gabe, and the co-pilot in amazement. They were all staring at *me* in amazement.

"Someone or something turned a light switch on in my mind," I said.

Out of curiosity, Madison asked, "Does your head hurt?"

"No, it's not like that," I replied. "But there is a lot of movement going on."

Madison looked at me and shook her head.

Gabe just stared and said, "No answers here."

With a real puzzled look, Austin said, "Must be a space thing?"

I really didn't expect them to provide an answer. However, the last person I expected an answer from was the co-pilot. I was surprised he even heard me, especially since he had returned to the cockpit. I thought he had turned his attention back to flying with the pilot. He must have been eavesdropping on our conversation. I guess he had gotten bored in the cockpit.

The co-pilot surprised me when he began to tell us a story about some bright, electric beings who looked like large bars of light. They were able to transform into other objects. That wasn't the kind of story I expected from an adult or a seasoned pilot. Perhaps he had seen or heard some things in his lifetime or in his profession as a pilot of an intergalactic spacecraft. It didn't hurt to listen to him. There was nothing else to do. There was no internet, and a bunch of downtime was staring at us before we reached Earth. An easygoing space story was a good companion. Besides, the story was a good replacement for all the drama and terror we had already experienced from a mere Earth game.

He could see his story was entertaining us, so he continued to talk about the men who had the appearance of bars of electric light. The Luminous Ones, as he called them, showed up throughout the universe but particularly on Earth. Their purpose was to bring wisdom, revelation, creativity, and lots of new inventions. According to him, the presence and influence of the Luminous Ones had grown on Earth. They were one of the reasons knowledge was rapidly increasing on Earth. He even gave them credit for all the new software inventions within the 20th and 21st centuries. *That's a stretch,* I thought.

In the beginning of his story, I wasn't really interested in it, but it was beginning to make sense. Supposedly, the Luminous Ones are always looking for someone who would cooperate with them to carry out new ideas and scientific inventions on Earth. *Why didn't we hear about them on the Top of the Universe?* The co-pilot continued to explain the purpose of the Luminous Ones.

"Have you noticed men have started traveling out in space again? Who or what do you think is drawing them out here? They didn't just, out of nowhere, wake up with the idea of space travel. The Luminous Ones download ideas and thoughts to keep civilizations progressing and advancing and to keep men and women moving closer and closer to the Top of the Universe."

"Are the Luminous Ones from the Top of the Universe?" I asked.

"Not exactly."

"Do they have a planet of their own?"

"They are not confined to one planet or universe," he responded.

"Can you see them with your naked eye?"

"Sometimes, yes. Sometimes no."

"Well, what's their origin?"

"The Top of the Universe"

"Do they talk?"

"Only when it's necessary."

"Why are they interested in Earth?"

"Earth is part of their assignment."

"What's the possibility of us seeing them? Are they any relation to the Watchmen? Hey, I am beginning to see quick streams of thoughts again."

I didn't wait for him to answer any of my questions. I just kept going like I couldn't stop.

The co-pilot was very patient as he answered my barrage of questions.

"A lot of people from space are coming to Earth, and a lot of people from Earth are trying to make it into space."

"Is this the last days or something? Or the beginning of the shadow of the first new Millennium? Is civilization about to go to the next stage? The universe is always expanding, so I guess it would be normal for everybody to start moving around, too."

The co-pilot's response caught me off guard when he said, "You kids are really smart. I thought you would have figured it out by now. There are tribes of Hosts."

"What!" I said. "Tribes!?"

"Yes. Tribes. The Luminous Ones are part of a tribe. Remember the Watchmen? They are part of a tribe, too."

"What about the tall, fierce, translucent, brown men dressed in shining armor? Who are they?"

"The Reinforcers."

"And who were the vicious dragonflies?"

"Just what you saw. Vicious dragonflies. You don't have to figure it out. They are just what you see and just what they do. Don't overthink it."

"If that's the case, who are you?"

"We are just what you see. Space pilots. Not astronauts. Astronauts explore. We know the terrain. We have a whole lot of information in our heads. The past, the present, the future, the galaxies, and the planets. We have been around for a long time and traveled through hundreds of galaxies."

"What do you know about Earth?"

"I know enough to know we need to get you back home before everyone figures out you are gone."

After listening to the co-pilot, I figured out a few things. One, he kept talking to me in generalities, nothing real specific. Second, he never told me what galaxy or planet he was from. If I didn't know better, with all his generalities, I would have assumed he didn't have a birthday or parents. Anyway, how do you account for another world that's different from your own?

Things don't necessarily always work the same way. Other than being a pilot, he really didn't tell us what his purpose was behind all these universal trips. He couldn't have been that shallow. If he had that much information about the galaxies, he had to have some unlimited storage capacity in his brain that was processing everything. He might be a robot on assignment, but not the kind of robot we imagine on Earth.

One thing I have learned from my journeys from Earth is . . . thoughts are limiting, and our thoughts transform us once we depart from Earth. I wanted the co-pilot to tell me how the Top of the Universe fit into all this. I knew he was associated with the Light of that planet because he took us straight to it.

"So, the Luminous Ones are just another tribe?" I asked.

"The Luminous Ones are hosts," he answered. "Hosts have lots of tribes within their groups. The tribe is assigned to help beings, especially teenagers. The Luminous Ones make their first contact with beings when they are teenagers. They revisit them throughout their lives. Illuminate. They bring light. That's what they do."

"How's that?" I asked.

"They bring a spirit of wisdom and revelation."

"What does that mean?"

"They enlighten, or reveal truth to, the eyes of men's understanding and help them to know their purpose."

"How does the light work with teenagers?"

"It's like a candle inside the soul. It brings light to what's already there. It stirs up and stimulates the desire for what's already inside of them . . . and what they were created to be and do."

"Have the Luminous hosts ever visited one of us on Earth before? Would we have known it?"

The co-pilot hesitated as if he wanted to keep a secret. Then he slowly spoke.

"I believe so."

He looked in Gabe's direction and said, "I see the light. I see the light inside you."

Gabe didn't act surprised. I thought he would have.

"You remember anything?" I asked.

It didn't take Gabe long to bring back the experience.

"Ahhh, I think I remember something. When I was thirteen, I went on a school trip far from my home. We visited an observatory located in the mountains. It had a large telescope. As I saw the stars and the planets in the sky through the telescope, I thought I saw a flying meteor in the sky. There was just one problem with that thought. It wasn't on fire like a meteor, and the closer it came to me, the more I realized it was a moving, bright light, like a large bar of streaming lights. Although it never reached me, it was in that moment that a warm presence came over me, and from that day on, I just felt like I belonged in the skies."

"That sounds like them, the Luminous Ones," said the co-pilot. "Your human spirit is like a lamp, searching and exposing all your innermost parts. The Luminous Ones help you see what was already there."

"Do the Luminous Ones ever alter things?"

"Yes. They impact civilizations and history. They bring light . . . and give light. When the light comes, it brings insight, wisdom, and revelations, and witty and creative ideas come."

"You said that before, but that's not what I had in mind," Madison said. "What about things like wars? Do they get involved?"

"No. That's not their purpose or assignment. There are specific host army warriors that combat wars and darkness. I haven't run across them in my travels.

"I have been traveling the universe for a while, and I have seen a lot. I saw the Luminous Ones during the Renaissance Age, the Industrial Age, and the start of the Information Age. They pay visits to people. When they arrive, they come with ideas. Some people take them and consider them, and the ideas take their lives and the world to the next level."

"What about the iPhone?" Madison said. "Did they have anything to do with the iPhone?"

"Yes. I saw them traveling with the idea. Changed things, didn't it?

"You remember George Washington Carver? Well, they were there in his lab when he created over 100 inventions at Tuskegee Institute. Remember the Dark Ages? When the enlightenment came, they were the ones that brought the light. The Luminous tribes visited artists and inventors, and from darkness, beauty, and new truths were unfolded. They helped create Renaissance art. People started thinking and imagining things again. That's what light brings. Light creates. That's why they are the Luminous Ones."

"So, the Luminous Ones are in front of destiny," Austin remarked. "Is there such a thing as Earth destiny?"

"Destiny is tied to the universe. It doesn't come from Earth. It's from the Top of the Universe. We are all moving forward and expanding and moving toward the Greater Light."

"What about darkness? What about those vicious dragonflies that attacked us?" Madison asked.

"They are deviants. They separated from the Light a long time ago and were expelled for their evil works. Concentrate on the Light. That's where real life and joy are," the co-pilot replied.

You could tell he didn't want to continue to talk about darkness, but Madison did. In fact, she asked another question.

"Where does the darkness live now?"

"I don't visit them or travel their way, and they are not on my radar. So I can't answer your question. Follow the Light you were shown on the Top of the Universe, and your path will become brighter and brighter by the day. In the brightness of your steps, you will be able to resist the darkness."

"Remember. The Hosts of tribes are drawing Earth toward the Top of the Universe more and more, and the hosts are increasing their visits to Earth. Keep your eyes, ears, and hearts open. By the way, sometimes the Luminous Ones and the other tribes transform into human beings."

For a split second, almost unnoticed, flickering, soft, blue lights appeared and then disappeared in the co-pilot's eyes. Then he turned back around and rejoined the pilot in flight.

CHAPTER 19

New Chapter

According to space-time, Serapha said we hadn't lost any Earth time back at home. That didn't matter to me. I just knew I'd been away from home for a very long time.

Shortly after we entered Earth's solar system, we were passing by Saturn. The rings around Saturn were so spectacular that Austin pulled his iPhone out of his pocket to take a picture of it. You might be wondering . . . why did Austin have an iPhone in his pocket this far out in space? Easy. He never thought he was going this far from home.

"Thanks for taking the picture, Austin," Gabe said. "Now we have proof that we were in outer space."

"Do we really want to tell everyone? Do we even want to tell *any*one? Who would believe us?" I asked.

Then Austin made a real good point.

"This is a game with reality mixed into it. This was our reality, so how could we make it real to someone else?" he said.

"We couldn't," I replied.

It was a tough call, but we all agreed that Austin was right.

If we told the wrong person about our Top of the Universe episode, they might say that we were crazy. We could end up in counseling for the next three years of our lives. So it was best to be quiet about the matter . . . at least for now.

Although we had agreed not to talk, inside our hearts, we had also agreed to carry out the blueprints we viewed in the Archives. The future vision of our lives on movie screens wasn't new to us. They were already in our hearts before we ever started the games. Serapha was important to us because she helped us realize the importance of our lives.

There was another message that Serapha and her friends . . . whomever they were . . . wanted us to carry back to Earth. The message was that science was important, and kids, youth, and adults needed to pay more attention to science so that our society would not decline.

In a matter of minutes, we were back at my house on Earth. The bluish-white, glimmering girl was right. We got back home on time . . . and no one seemed to miss us. Space-time and the Top of the Universe time were different from Earth's time. After going through winter, spring, summer, Mars, and, let's not forget, Neptune, it was still Thursday evening. No one noticed we had been gone, not even the dog. Austin's parents had just pulled into our driveway. Austin's mother was there to pick Madison and him up.

Friday was kind of sad for me. It was Gabe's last day in America. Gabe showed his appreciation to my family by inviting us to come to Brazil the next summer. I accepted his offer, but my father didn't.

Gabe didn't waste any time jumping into his future. At five o'clock in the evening, we escorted him to the airport. He put his captain's pilot cap on right before he walked through the airport. He had enough sense to wait until my father turned away before he put the cap on his head.

All eyes were on Gabe as he strutted through the airport's gate and onto the plane with his captain's cap. Although it was make-believe, he still felt good. He looked like a kid with a dream, and he knew it. He just smiled back at everyone as if he was "the man." The flight crew treated Gabe special when he boarded the plane because they gathered that he wanted to be one of them one day. By the way, an authentic captain's pilot cap isn't exactly a souvenir from America.

Spring break was just about over. We had learned enough lessons to last us for the rest of the school year. The lessons from the Top of the Universe were tucked neatly away in the back of our minds. Once we were back in school, we had a new enthusiasm and excitement for learning science.

As a team, Madison, Austin, and I decided to embrace Austin's theme, "Science, the New Cool", as a way of life. It didn't take long for us to persuade the whole school to follow us. Mr. Matthews and the school principal were ecstatic over our new science campaign.

Within a week, the principal had over 700 purple T-shirts printed that read "Science, the New Cool." Madison, Austin, and I were the first students to wear the shirts. Everyone wanted to know what the slogan meant. However, they didn't find out until the principal called a special school assembly to promote the new campaign.

We were invited to join the principal on stage in the school's auditorium as we kicked off the "Science, the New Cool" campaign. Mr. Matthews joined us on stage, too. The school's administrators and teachers decided to create a special video presentation for the science rally. Believe it or not, they asked us to help write the video presentation. We used the same screen script we saw in the presentation on the Top of the Universe's Archive Room. The development committee was really impressed with our ideas.

The principal said, "Those ideas were out of this world. You youth really have a vision for what we need to do in this school . . . and in this nation." Another adult who was on the development committee just looked at us and asked, "Who's your momma and daddy?"

The principal got real worked up about the new science campaign. "Worked up" is an understatement. He made the whole concept a revival. Maybe he needed a revival, a new reason for being principal. Maybe he needed something to break his normal routine.

Principals spend most of every day putting out fires and trying to make schools better. However, who would have ever thought our principal wanted to be a crusader for a cause? Instead of just having a mini-presentation on the contributions of science and why science was important, he turned it into a school-wide science fair. Along with the school's science projects, there was information from science in the past and in the future.

Now, everyone has a boss. My parents are my boss. For the principal, the superintendent of schools is his boss. When the superintendent heard what our principal was doing, he decided to make it a citywide campaign at all schools; elementary, middle, and high school, too!

The movement had taken on a life of its own. "Science, the New Cool" became the revival subject of our city. And we were the spokespersons. We understood that science wasn't just cool; it was necessary and essential for everyday living.

Madison, Austin, and I went from being ordinary high school students to examples. It was good that we didn't have a big ego or an inflated opinion of ourselves, or else our heads would have been real big by now.

Friends weren't hard to find anymore, either. In fact, everyone wanted to hang with us now and be a part of our clique. Nevertheless, Madison, Austin, and I still stuck together. We were the glue that mattered, that kept our friendship tight. Our friendship had substance and respect. However, we were the new "it" kids in the school. And to think that all this started with the delivery of a telescope.

We still don't know who delivered it and what their motivation was. The mysterious telescope was a defining moment in our lives . . . and a turning point.

Furthermore, even Lawrence, the school bully, was trying to be friends with us. I cut a deal with him. In exchange for my friendship, I told him I would be seen in public with him if he signed a contract to stop bullying students. There had to be restitution or repayment for bad behavior, so I required him to tutor students for ten straight weeks. I did this because I wanted to send three messages to the other students about him. The messages were: He was a changed man. He wanted to make things right. He was capable of being a friend. Wow. I felt like I had really stepped into my purpose and was already doing my part to help make the world a better place… or Crossings High School, anyway.

The local and national television news stations became involved in our "Science, the New Cool" campaign. The campaign took on a life of its own. The smallest event or rumble breathed new fire and life into our campaign all over again.

Over 1,000,000 science tweets were received in one day. The tweets kept coming. The "Science, the New Cool" campaign had spread across the United States. Kids were getting excited about science? Staying up all night working on science projects? Spending their allowance for science kits instead of video games?

Anonymous multi-millionaires were coming out of the closet trying to get in on the new science momentum. One 80-year-old billionaire got dressed up, put on a suit, and arrived at our school unexpectedly and made a donation of over $500,000. After the excitement was over about the massive donation, we learned that the donor was a retired scientist.

Money was pouring in from everywhere to schools all across the country to boost science classes, science research, and science clubs. Kids started going on science field trips again. Science labs were being expanded in elementary, middle, and high schools throughout the nation. Science projects, inventions, and discoveries were applauded and posted throughout the walls of America's schools and in libraries everywhere.

Adults, teenagers, and even kids started coming up with all kinds of witty inventions and discoveries. It was crazy. There were so many new inventions coming from schools that new stores with all kinds of new science products and kits were popping up everywhere. The country's economy was being boosted every month. It was off the chain!

Technology, science, and simple inventions had become such hot topics in America that corporate executives and venture capitalists, who fund new businesses and new ideas, were visiting middle schools and high schools in search of new ideas and projects to fund.

Business executives were showing up from all over the nation wearing gym shoes. I saw one man running into a school to get in line for a science fair. Adults were lining up for ideas and concepts like kids had lined up to get into Mervin Matthews' game store. It was wild!

Our teacher, Mr. Matthews, was so on top of his game. He had become a key figure in the big to-do about science. He was finally able to share his love and passion for science with the whole country. "Science, the New Cool" was no longer just a campaign. Science *was* now really cool in America.

The campaign had taken all of us further than we planned to go and kept us longer than we planned to stay. The campaign moved to a new level, and we moved with it. Instead of just appearing in school auditoriums and in the local news, we were now being paraded to a national stage. We were invited to places like Miami, FL, and Austin, TX.

Madison, Austin, Mr. Matthews, and I were the sought-after speakers for "Science, the New Cool" campaign. Other organizations, famous people, and everyday people had taken up the cause. However, for their special events, they wanted us to be present. I guess our presence brought a sense of genuineness and made their events bona fide and legitimate.

Our parents were getting concerned about us being away from home so much. My mother, however, came up with a new perspective regarding our time away. She said the times we went out of town and attended special events added up to the same amount of time we had spent playing video games before. Frankly speaking, she welcomed the change. My mom had a favorite and consistent saying about video games in our house.

She used to constantly say, "I am tired of you playing those games; I wish you would do something more constructive with your life."

Well, now we were, and she was loving it.

My mom's attitude and comments were not unique. Parents throughout America were beginning to say the same thing. It was a welcomed change, and they were able to see something constructive in their kids' preoccupation with science projects. Video games had been the enemy. But little did they know that it was the games that had led us to our destiny. We were captured by the games. The games had brought us to our destiny.

CHAPTER 20

Origins

The national science campaign caused Mr. Matthews to mature beyond his natural age. The extra responsibility and work didn't seem to matter, though, because he loved his new role. He had become the spokesperson for the "Science, the New Cool" campaign. He was in demand. Although it might be hard to believe, because of the added responsibilities and duties, he wasn't absent from class a lot, and neither were we. As a matter of fact, he actually started giving us more quizzes and tests on a regular basis. Maybe he wanted to demonstrate to us he was more than "just show" now. We got his point.

Can you believe that after all of the publicity, Mr. Mathews still gave us special assignments during the weekends, too? Some things never change. At least the guy was consistent. Even though he likes him a lot, Austin was overwhelmed by last weekend's assignment.

"Mr. Matthews got a little crazy inside of him," Austin remarked. "I can see how he and his twin brother are related. They are both extremists. They don't do anything halfway."

I wasn't going to take his over-the-top homework assignments that far. Mervin Matthews, however, was a different subject. We did arrive at the conclusion that he *was* legitimately crazy and that he had issues that both you and I know about.

Speaking of Mervin Matthews, he was keeping a low profile, like a person in hiding who had done something wrong. After all the press we were receiving (we being Mr. Mathews, Madison, Austin, and I), Mervin Matthews still had not been spotted at *any* award ceremony or at any special conference. Out of the hundreds of participants, supporters of the cause, and well-wishers regarding the "Science, the New Cool" campaign, Mr. Matthews' brother had never shown up once.

It's possible that Mervin Matthews had some governmental restrictions on what he could and couldn't do. One restriction might have had something to do with schools. It seemed that schools were off-limits to him for sure. Whatever he did, it sure was being kept quiet. What's even more interesting is that although a group of United States Air Force personnel had escorted him out of the school, the event never made it to the internet or the television news. Following his first all-star year as the new Crossings High School science teacher and six months on the "Science, the New Cool" tour, Mr. Matthews finally got his full due. He received the "Teacher of the Year" award. And that's a really big thing.

The president of the United States called Mr. Matthews to the White House. Mr. Matthews didn't want to go alone, so he asked Madison, Austin, and me to accompany him. Quite naturally, we all wore our new "Science, the New Cool" purple shirts. Mr. Matthews wore his only suit. To think, all of this happened less than a year after we returned from the Top of the Universe.

Our lives had returned back to normal, but we still remembered our *life-changing* trip to the Top of the Universe, and we remembered Serapha, the blue, singing, and dancing girl who helped bring meaning to our lives. In our minds and hearts, we wished we could have brought Serapha into our present world. She was our friend for life. But she wasn't in our world now . . . least not physically.

A real friend makes your life better. They help you see and understand yourself. They know your good times and help you through the bad times, and they usually stick around through both the good and the bad. And you never forget a real, true friend.

Today was President's Day, our day with the president of the United States of America. We were standing on a stage in a room full of people who were smiling at us. When the president walked out to meet us, we felt real important . . . because we were. Mr. Matthews, Madison, and I were caught up in the moment of the event. It was a great moment in our lives. But Austin was checking out the security team around the president. Austin, like Gabe, was jumping into his future. We should have expected it.

The four of us received the "Distinguished Service Award in Education" from the president of the United States. The award was for our "Science, the New Cool" campaign. A classroom of high school youth from the area was positioned throughout the audience to ensure that it looked like a school event instead of a government event. Most of the kids looked like they were glad to have a day off from school, but they still seemed proud of us.

On the way back from Washington, D. C. something special happened. We were gazing out of the window of the plane, and there appeared a shaft of pure, radiant blue light. The moment the radiant blue light appeared, we knew it was our friend, Serapha. She was glimmering outside the plane's window. We couldn't see her face, but we knew it was her. She was a welcomed sight. Something inside us felt good knowing that she had not forgotten about us. As a result of our friendship with her, our lives had become greater and more meaningful.

We were living beyond ourselves. We had surpassed our normal human reasoning. She had caused us, at a young age, to ride upon the high places of the Earth and stand with the leaders of our nation. The floodgates of our minds were opened to the new life of the universe. We didn't feel like mere human beings anymore, let alone normal teenagers. And we weren't. Our minds had been renewed. We had a fresh mental attitude.

We had assumed that our lives were moving faster because of what occurred in our minds while we rode the Top of the Universe's lightning-fast horses. But that wasn't it. Life was moving faster, and we were having great success because we were living out the blue-print for our lives. We had stepped into the picture frame. The frame had life and energy within itself.

If you are like me, somewhere in the back of your mind, you are still wondering where Mr. Matthews' brother, Mervin, was. What happened to him? After all, he did introduce us to the video game that took us through the solar systems and to the Top of the Universe.

Serapha returned into our lives, but Mr. Matthews' brother didn't. Surely, Mervin Matthews has read about us on the internet or has seen us on the evening television news or on the cover of the newspapers. You think!

Maybe it was enough for Mervin Matthews to know we had survived the games. Gabe always maintained that he was monitoring our every move. Come to think of it . . . does Mr. Matthews' brother even talk to him? Most people talk about their family whether they like them or not, but not our teacher, Mr. Matthews. What's up with the Matthews family?

While we were wondering what Mervin Matthews was doing and thinking, Austin started eavesdropping on him. I really shouldn't have told you this. Eavesdropping, particularly wiretapping, is illegal.

We chalked it up by saying, "We all knew that Austin would be head of a national and international computer security organization one day."

Austin put his espionage skills into practice. By doing this, he solved the ongoing mystery of Mervin Matthews. Why did Mervin Matthews have a video game store? What was the top secret that he learned at NASA? Why hadn't he contacted us? And why was he escorted from the school?

For the past two months, without telling anyone, Austin had secretly wiretapped Mervin Matthews' personal phone line and hacked into his computers. Don't ask me how he did this. If I told you how he did it, I would become an accomplice to a crime. On May 10th, almost six months after our return from the Top of the Universe, Austin overheard a conversation that answered all our questions about Mr. Matthews' brother.

"Hello, Mr. Matthews. This is the president of the United States. Good job! Mission accomplished. Our nation is back on track. Our schools, military, technology, security systems, and way of life will be secure in the future. And, by the way, get rid of that game."

Mervin Matthews responded, "Will do, sir. Right away"

"We appreciate your service to the country," replied the president.

"Thank you, Mr. President. Isn't it amazing how video games have served our country?"

Our trip to the Top of the Universe, the video games, and the mysterious telescope were all part of a top-secret mission to redirect and increase students' interest in science. They were stepping stones for good. The "Science, the New Cool" campaign and Mervin Matthews' secret mission were good ideas. But wouldn't it have been just as easy to have trained and hired a lot more teachers like Mr. Matthews?

I guess teachers like Mr. Matthews are hard to come by. They're probably aren't a lot of them around. I guess we did need a science campaign to make up the difference for what was inside our teacher.

After all of this... you would never believe what Austin said to me.

"Mr. Matthews' brother isn't crazy after all. Maybe they should let him teach kids again." In complete unbelief, I shouted, "No way! There are still standards. Besides, those three Crossings High School boys who disappeared still haven't returned to Earth yet. They were certainly ready to return as model citizens. Who knows? We might find them on our next journey, representing American kids in Australia, South America . . . even in another galaxy." This was the end for now, or at least until Mervin Matthews surfaces again.

Then I turned my head, and to my surprise and delight, Serapha was standing not too far away and staring at me from a distance . . . shining and smiling. This time she was much larger in stature, and her shape appeared to flow and transform like a massive cloud that blends into the air. By now, I realized she was greater than life, and the origin of life had ordered her into our lives in the most awesome way.

ABOUT THE AUTHOR

C. A. Mickels is a first-time author. Her background includes working in private education settings, which has given her insight into the fascinating and intricate world of youth. Magnetic Pulls is merely the beginning of an awe-inspiring journey into the depths of youth's untapped potential—a journey that promises to touch lives, inspire dreams, and instill a sense of wonderment in every soul it reaches. Mickels is a graduate of the University of Michigan.

cb305f6f-4820-40fa-9818-f2ce42b94a7bR01